*"We'...

but we plan to interview a lot of people,"
Chas Brewster said, gently discouraging her
because he couldn't imagine this woman caring
for triplets who required round-the-clock care.

Lily Andersen nodded.

Gazing at her, Chas acknowledged that nature
had truly outdone itself when it created this
woman. Lily was the kind of beautiful that stopped
traffic. For a good ten seconds, Chas wished she
really did want to play mother to three motherless
children, but he squelched that wish because it
was selfish. Right now his top priority had to be
the health, safety and well-being of the children.
Besides, this gorgeous blue-eyed blonde was about
the furthest thing from a nanny he'd ever seen.

He couldn't have a relationship with her. First, if
he hired her, she'd be his employee. Second, if he
hired her, she'd be living in his house.

Both spelled trouble.

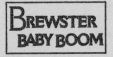

BREWSTER BABY BOOM

Dear Reader,

Not only is February the month for lovers, it is the second month for readers to enjoy exciting celebratory titles across all Silhouette series. Throughout 2000, Silhouette Books will be commemorating twenty years of publishing the best in contemporary category romance fiction. This month's Silhouette Romance lineup continues our winning tradition.

Carla Cassidy offers an emotional VIRGIN BRIDES title, in which a baby on the doorstep sparks a second chance for a couple who'd once been *Waiting for the Wedding*—their own!—and might be again.... Susan Meier's charming miniseries BREWSTER BABY BOOM continues with *Bringing Up Babies*, as black sheep brother Chas Brewster finds himself falling for the young nanny hired to tend his triplet half siblings.

A beautiful horse trainer's quest for her roots leads her to two men in Moyra Tarling's *The Family Diamond. Simon Says... Marry Me!* is the premiere of Myrna Mackenzie's THE WEDDING AUCTION. Don't miss a single story in this engaging three-book miniseries. A pregnant bride-for-hire dreams of making *The Double Heart Ranch* a real home, but first she must convince her husband in this heart-tugger by Leanna Wilson. And *If the Ring Fits...* some lucky woman gets to marry a prince! In this sparkling debut Romance from Melissa McClone, an accident-prone American heiress finds herself a royal bride-to-be!

In coming months, look for Diana Palmer, a Joan Hohl-Kasey Michaels duet and much more. It's an exciting year for Silhouette Books, and we invite you to join the celebration!

Happy Reading!

Mary-Theresa Hussey

Mary-Theresa Hussey
Senior Editor

Please address questions and book requests to:
Silhouette Reader Service
U.S.: 3010 Walden Ave., P.O. Box 1325, Buffalo, NY 14269
Canadian: P.O. Box 609, Fort Erie, Ont. L2A 5X3

BRINGING UP BABIES

Susan Meier

Silhouette
ROMANCE™
Published by Silhouette Books
America's Publisher of Contemporary Romance

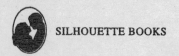

SILHOUETTE BOOKS

ISBN 0-373-19427-7

BRINGING UP BABIES

Visit us at www.romance.net

Printed in U.S.A.

Books by Susan Meier

Silhouette Romance

Stand-in Mom #1022
Temporarily Hers #1109
Wife in Training #1184
Merry Christmas, Daddy #1192
*In Care of the Sheriff #1283
*Guess What? We're Married! #1338
Husband from 9 to 5 #1354
*The Rancher and the Heiress #1374
†The Baby Bequest #1420
†Bringing Up Babies #1427

*Texas Family Ties
†Brewster Baby Boom

Silhouette Desire

Take the Risk #567

SUSAN MEIER

has written category romances for Silhouette Romance and Silhouette Desire. A full-time writer now, Susan has also been an employee of a major defense contractor, a columnist for a small newspaper and a division manager of a charitable organization. But the greatest joy in her life has always been her children, who constantly surprise and amaze her. Married for twenty years to her wonderful, understanding and gorgeous husband, Michael, Susan cherishes her roles as a mother, wife, sister and friend, believing them to be life's real treasures. She not only cherishes those roles as gifts, she tries to convey the beauty and importance of loving relationships in her books.

Chas:

Because you seem to have a little difficulty understanding the wisdom of your heart, I'm going to pass on the advice of my own father. Opposites will always attract. Not just because there's fun in trying to figure out how to get along, but also because opposites complement each other. Stop looking for someone who is as smart as you are or as determined as you are, and start looking for someone who knows how to relax and let life lead her where she's destined to go—someone who knows how to be as happy with a little as she can be with a lot.

And let her into your heart. Don't just give her money and the promise of a position and power—show her the enormous capacity for love that you guard like a buried treasure. Because it is a treasure to be at the same time vulnerable yet strong. A good woman will understand and appreciate that.

If you find that woman, don't ever let her go.

Love,

Dad

Chapter One

"Hi, I'm Lily Andersen. You advertised for a nanny?"

Chas Brewster stared in amazement at the woman standing at his front door. The gorgeous blue-eyed blonde was about the farthest thing from a nanny he'd ever seen.

"Yes. Come in," he said, then swallowed hard. With her big, bright sapphire eyes and bounty of luxurious yellow curls accenting the peaches and cream complexion of her face, Lily Andersen had the kind of beauty that could stop traffic. She wore a baby-blue sweater that wasn't designed to accent her bosom, but did anyway, and modest jeans covering a perfect derriere and long legs.

"We're looking for a nanny, but we plan to interview a lot of people," he said, gently discouraging her because he couldn't imagine this woman caring for triplet babies who required nearly round-the-clock care. "For first interviews I'm only asking a few preliminary questions. Suitable candidates will be called back for a second interview."

Lily nodded her understanding. Chas motioned to the right, directing her down the hall to the den, praising the heavens as he followed behind her. Watching her hips move he acknowledged that nature had truly outdone itself when it created this woman. For a good ten seconds he wished she really did want to play mother to three motherless children, but he squelched that wish because it was selfish. Right now his top priority had to be the health, safety and well-being of the children.

Besides, he couldn't have a relationship with her, anyway. First, if he hired her, she'd be his employee. Second, if he hired her, she'd be living in his house. Both circumstances spelled trouble.

Taking another look at the subtle swing of her hips, Chas sighed. It was a fun fantasy while it had lasted.

"Second door on the right," he said.

She turned and smiled. "Thank you."

Chas instructed Lily to take a seat as he rounded the old, worn desk that had once been his father's to sit on the battered burgundy leather chair behind it. Professionally, as if he had interviewed nannies a million times, he reached for his legal pad and pen. "You said your name was Lily Anderson," he said, writing the information at the top of the page.

"That's right. Lily Andersen. *A-N-D-E-R-S-E-N,* not *O-N.*"

Chas glanced up and smiled. *"E-N,"* he repeated, making the note, though he knew the record would be worthless. When she discovered the job was caring for triplets, not one child, she would probably run in the other direction, but more than that, he'd already figured out he couldn't seriously consider her a candidate to care for Taylor, Cody and Antoinette, whom they called Annie, unless she had excellent credentials. Tamping down the thought that it would be nice to simply *look* at this woman twenty-four hours a day, he knew her ability to attend to the children was the real bottom line.

"Where are you from, Lily?"

"Wisconsin."

That stopped him. "You're an awfully long way from home."

She shrugged carelessly. "I know. I was feeling stifled by my family and decided to get away."

"To Pennsylvania?" he asked incredulously.

She grinned charmingly, innocently. "Why not?"

Confused, Chas only stared at her. If she were running away, he'd expect a woman of her good looks to choose a place like Los Angeles or New York, a place where she might be able to put those good looks to work as an actress or model.

"I love Pennsylvania," she continued. "You have beautiful mountains and fabulous trees. For a mid-Atlantic state, Pennsylvania has kept a lot of its rural appeal. I could probably live here happily forever."

The flowing, melodious tones of her lovely voice lulled him into a warm, comfortable state and he found himself gazing at her like a love-sick puppy. She was beautiful, her voice was soft and sexy, and she had an absolutely perfect figure....

Call him a chauvinist, but a man had to know the limits of his endurance, and Chas knew his. Having this woman living with him in this house wasn't going to work.

He almost felt bad for rejecting her for a problem that was his, not hers—then he realized the problem could be hers. Rather than believe she wanted to live in the middle of nowhere, it made more sense to think she was on her way to the big city, needed money, saw the Brewster ad, decided she could make quick, easy cash and stopped to try to get the job.

Well, that was the end of that. He didn't have to worry about being overwhelmingly attracted to her anymore. Not only was she too beautiful to run after three screaming, hungry babies, who demanded full-time attention, but she was a transient. There was no way he'd introduce the children to a nanny who would desert them after a few weeks, or even a few months. Given the way they'd been shuffled around, these kids needed someone more permanent.

He cleared his throat. "Yes, well, I certainly love Pennsylvania, too," he said, then pretended to consult some notes. He would ask a few more general questions as a formality, then, with a clear conscience, he'd send her on her way. "Tell me about your child-care experience."

"Who cares about her child-care experience?" Grant, Chas's oldest brother, said from the door of the den. Cradling their baby brother and two sisters in his well-muscled forearms, dark-haired, bearded Grant walked into the room. "For some reason or another, Chas, I get the impression you've forgotten we're desperate. At this point, I'm willing to take anybody."

"Oh, my gosh!" Lily exclaimed, jumping from her chair. "Aren't they the most adorable babies!"

All three of the kids wore one-piece rompers. The girls' were solid pink with a bunny appliqué on the chest. Cody's was gray with a multicolored train. Cody and Annie had sandy hair and light green eyes, but Taylor had dark hair and brown eyes. Looking at the eight-month-old triplets the way a stranger would, Chas had to admit that, yes, they were adorable.

"Don't let their looks deceive you," he said, aware that he was behaving like a man dousing water on the fire, but also knowing it was for the best. These kids needed more than a temporary nanny. "At three o'clock in the afternoon, well rested from their naps, they seem adorable. At three o'clock in the morning, hungry and wanting to play rather than sleep, they are as far from adorable as you can get."

"Oh, they are not!" Lily said, taking Taylor from Grant's outstretched arms. "Look at you," she said, brushing her cheek against Taylor's in a gesture of complete fascination with the little girl with the dark hair and eyes like Grant's. "You're just precious."

"They're all precious and wonderful," Grant said as he slid Cody and Annie into the play yard set up in the den for Chas's convenience when he had to work. "And surprisingly easy to care for."

Chas's eyes bugged out in astonishment. "You're lying," he said without thinking.

Grant glared at him. "These children are a joy to have around."

"These children are *family*," Chas said. "And I love all three of them dearly, but they are not always a joy to have around."

Grant thrust his chin in Lily's direction, then tried to send Chas a message with his eyes.

Chas frowned and shook his head.

"Well, they're beautiful children," Lily said, stroking Cody's cheek while she balanced Taylor on her hip. "And they appear to be very well behaved." She smiled at Grant, then Chas. "Whose babies are they?"

Chas looked at Grant. Grant looked at Chas. Finally

Chas said, "They belonged to our father and stepmother, both of whom died recently. Grant and I, along with our brother, Evan, were granted custody."

"Oh, so the three of you live in this house?" Lily questioned innocently.

"No, our brother Evan got married over the weekend. He's on his honeymoon," Grant said.

"Which leaves the two of you as guardians for the kids," Lily surmised, glancing from brother to brother.

Chas shook his head. "No. We recognized that each child needed individualized attention, and we've all more or less adopted a child to be our own. The kids stay together all day, then in the evening I take care of Annie, Evan and Claire will have Cody, and Grant gets Taylor."

Lily shot him a confused expression, but Chas decided that was good. She might be sweet, she might be nice, she might even have honorable intentions about trying to care for kids, but he suspected she was only here temporarily. He wasn't about to hire somebody who wouldn't stay around.

"So, what you're telling me, then, is that the job is more of a daytime thing?"

"And we're planning to hire a housekeeper," Grant said encouragingly.

"You simply want someone to care for the children?"

"Absolutely," Grant said, grinning charmingly.

"Eventually," Chas contradicted sternly. "For now the nanny will have to do basic housekeeping, and the job is at least ten hours a day," Chas reminded, again bringing everything back to reality. "Because you'd be the primary care giver, there will be times we'll expect you to baby-sit in the evenings. There will also be times *you* would be responsible for overnight duty. Grant's in the process of bringing his construction company north and once it's here he'll need a full night's sleep. I'm setting up my law practice. I won't always have to get up first thing in the morning, but when I do, I'll also need my sleep.''

"But the nanny will have a room upstairs for convenience in caring for the kids,'' Grant put in immediately. "You'll live here. Room and board is part of the package. Afternoons or mornings that you're not needed will be your free time. We'll try to work out advance schedules,'' he added, skewering Chas with a look that dared him to try to throw water on that one.

"It sounds like exactly what I'm looking for,'' Lily began, but Chas stopped her.

"That's great,'' he said, rising from his seat to walk around the desk. He placed his hand on the small of her back and guided her to the door. "Like I said, once I've completed all the first interviews, I'll begin calling people back for second interviews. I do have a number where you can be reached, don't I?''

"I'm staying at the bed and breakfast on Main Street,'' Lily said, handing Taylor to Grant. "If you want me for a second interview, just call Abby, I guess.''

"Okay. Fine. That's great,'' Chas said as he directed her out.

He got as far as the door before Grant said, "What in the hell are you talking about first interviews and second interviews for? We are desperate. *Desperate.* I want somebody here tomorrow. I'm supposed to be in Savannah on Thursday. I'm not going to make it if we don't get some help soon.''

Chas tried to silence Grant with a glare, and Lily took a step forward out of the way of the two tall, angry, obviously disagreeing men. Dressed in a plaid work shirt and jeans, Grant was frightening and imposing, but Chas was majestic. His sandy-brown hair was straight but cut short and styled in such a way that not even one strand was out of place. His green eyes were clear, direct. Even wearing casual tan slacks and an open-necked yellow shirt, tall, whipcord-lean Chas had the look of a person in power. It could have been the way he carried himself. It could have been the fact that he didn't back down from his older, brawnier brother. Or it could have been because he seemed to be the one calling the shots.

Lily also wasn't surprised Chas didn't want her. She'd seen disapproval in his pale gray-green eyes the minute he opened the door to her. Men always had one of two reactions to her. They either thought she was a bubble brain or they thought she was riffraff.

Dignified, stately Chas apparently thought she wasn't good enough for his family.

"Grant, why don't we let Ms. Andersen go, and you and I will discuss this privately?" Chas asked.

"Why don't we let Ms. Andersen wait in the living room while I convince you you're an idiot, and that way I won't have to drive to town to apologize to her and beg her to take this job," Grant quickly countered.

Because Lily had been down roads like this one many times, she stepped in before the dispute became ugly. "Okay, look, I'm not going to pull any punches here." She faced Chas. "You think that because I'm blond I'm stupid," she said, opting for the nicer of the two choices for why Chas immediately disliked her. "Since I know I'm not, and since I know I'll do a very good job as nanny for your children and you'll be glad you hired me, I would be more than happy to work out some sort of a trial period."

Lily watched Grant smirk cockily and cross his arms

on his broad chest as if he knew her argument had won the battle, but she nonetheless held her breath waiting for Chas's reply. She might be staying at the B&B tonight and maybe tomorrow night, but basically that was all she could afford. She had to find a job today. Because it was already three o'clock, nanny to the Brewster children might be her salvation.

Chas sighed heavily. "Ms. Andersen, it isn't that I don't think you're capable of caring for the kids. I'm afraid you'll only be temporary."

She gave him a puzzled frown. "What do you mean?"

"Well, your home is awfully far away. What's to say you're not going to get homesick and just pick up and leave?"

Lily answered without a second's hesitation. "I won't."

When he didn't immediately respond, Lily knew her first guess was right on the money. Though he might truly question whether or not she'd stay in this town, that wasn't the real reason he didn't want to hire her. Since she couldn't defend his possible opinion of her social status, she chose to defend her abilities.

"My sister is ten years older than I am, and she had three babies in three years. Not only did I live with her after our mother died, but I baby-sat while she worked." She caught Chas's gaze and held it. "I can handle three kids. I've already done it."

"She's got you, Counselor," Grant said with a laugh.

"All right, a trial period," Chas said as if he were doing her a supreme favor. "But these babies are very important to us," he warned soberly. "If you don't do an excellent job and I do mean *excellent,* you're out. Do you understand me?"

"Oh, I understand you very, very well, Mr. Brewster," Lily said, giving Chas a pointed warning look of her own, before she turned to walk out of the den. "I'm going into town to get my things from Abby's. Please have my room ready when I return," she said, then left.

"I guess she told you," Grant said with a laugh after Lily was gone.

"I should punch you for getting us into this mess," Chas said, striding back to his chair behind the big desk.

"Punch me? Punch *me?* You were about to let the only nanny to answer our ad walk out the door. We've had that ad in the paper for months, and not one person answered it until Lily."

"Someone will come along eventually."

"Oh, yeah, right," Grant said and fell to the seat in front of Chas's desk. "No one wants this job. Face it, Chas, you are in rural Pennsylvania now. This isn't Philly. Nannies aren't flocking here in droves."

"Still, that doesn't mean we have to take the first person who comes along, either. Do you know you hired her before I had a chance to get references?"

"So, we'll get references when she returns."

"And what if we find out she's wanted for a felony in Wisconsin? What do we do then?"

"Then we let her go. That's what trial periods are for."

Chas dropped to his chair in exasperation. "All this is so easy for you because you're going to be out of town. What if she's careless or persnickety? What if she can't handle all three kids alone?"

"She's not going to be alone. It was never our plan to leave the nanny alone with the kids for long stretches of time. That's why you're setting up shop at the house, Counselor," Grant reminded archly. "You volunteered to be the watcher and helper so that Evan would have the freedom to take over the mill.''

"Yeah, and what are you supposed to be doing while I'm the watcher and helper?''

"I'm supposed to be bringing my very successful construction company up from Savannah, remember?'' Grant said, reaching out to lift Taylor from the play yard when she began to cry. He snuggled her against his neck, then sighed and said, "Come on, Chas, we need her. Period. End of story. At least until Evan gets back from his honeymoon. When Evan gets back we'll hold another meeting, maybe regroup and change our plans, but for now it's just you and me. And I have to go to Savannah.''

"So, go. I'll take care of the kids.''

"I'm not leaving you with three babies and no helper. Besides, Lily looks very capable to me.''

Chas gave him an incredulous stare. "Oh, yeah. She *looks* capable, all right.''

"What? You think because she's pretty she can't take care of kids?''

"No, I think that because she's pretty she's got bigger fish to fry than being nanny for the children of two bachelors in the wilds of Pennsylvania. Use your head, Grant, she's probably going to New York and we're a convenient stop along the way. A place where she can rest and earn some extra cash.''

Having settled Taylor, Grant rose from his chair. "I don't care if she is only temporary. She's solving an immediate problem. As far as I'm concerned that's good enough.''

He turned to walk out the door, but Chas called him back. "Grant, one of these days you're going to have to start thinking about the future.''

Grant laughed. "Not as long as I have you around.''

* * *

Lily got into her car and drove down the winding road that led into town, not even noticing the September breeze that rippled through the multicolored leaves of the dense forest around her. She couldn't stop thinking about Chas Brewster and had to struggle not to close her eyes in frustration, wishing for the one millionth time in her life that she'd gone to college as her sister had advised. At the time she'd thought Mary Louise had only been trying to be a good guardian, pointing out all Lily's options before Lily committed to helping her sister with her boys. Now she knew Mary Louise understood that pretty blondes didn't always get the respect they deserved. At least if she had a degree, no one could argue her abilities.

Lily sighed. But she hadn't wanted a degree. She'd wanted babies. She'd wanted to marry Everett, settle down in a suburban home and be a mom. She'd wanted to car pool to Little League games and ballet recitals. She'd wanted to sew Halloween costumes and give out candy to children for trick or treat. She'd also wanted to be the respected confidante of a man who would be her best friend, her partner, her companion and her lover. She'd wanted to give advice, talk out difficulties, plan the futures of her children and enjoy every second of her life—good or bad. Because she had genuinely believed there was nothing better, nothing more wonderful or more important than spending your life giving love, receiving love and teaching others to love.

Lily sighed heavily and maneuvered her car around a particularly sharp curve.

What a fool she'd been.

Betrayal had quickly stolen all her dreams, and time

hadn't given her the opportunity to come up with an alternate plan. But she did know one thing, she would never base her dreams on something so delicate as another person's affections. Not ever again.

She would take the job as the Brewster nanny and begin squirreling away her money, because eventually she was going to have to make some decisions about her life, some real decisions. If nothing else, she was going to have to find a way to support herself, because she didn't think Chas Brewster was going to keep her forever.

In fact, she knew he wouldn't.

Lily arrived at Brewster Mansion about two hours later. Her car was packed with every single thing she'd collected in her twenty-three years. Holding a suitcase in one hand and balancing a box on the other, she rang the doorbell.

Chas answered. "Come in, Lily," he said, sounding more resigned than glad to see her, though at least he was polite. He led her through the marble-floored foyer, through the immaculate all-white kitchen with the butcher-block counter in the center and to the door of what was probably maid's quarters.

He opened the door to a room that was twice the size of any living space Lily had ever had. "Oh, it's beautiful," she said before she had a chance to temper her reaction.

"I'm glad you like it. Go in, get settled, then come back to the den whenever you're ready, and we'll discuss salary."

Smiling brightly, Lily nodded. With one curt bob of his head Chas turned to leave and ran smack-dab into his older brother's broad chest.

"Why are you putting her down here?" Grant asked incredulously.

Lily watched as Chas directed Grant out of the small alcove in front of her room and closed her door, but he and Grant apparently didn't get any farther than the kitchen because she could hear them talking.

"This is where we agreed she'd stay."

"Yeah, I know, but I'm leaving, remember? I need my sleep tonight, which means you'll need help with those babies."

"I'll take care of the kids."

"I'm sure you'll try," Grant agreed, "but I'm also sure you'll fail. So put her upstairs, as close to those kids as you can get her."

Obviously exasperated, Chas sarcastically said, "What do you want me to do, put her in my room?"

There was a pause, a long one. When Grant replied, there was laughter in his voice. "Do *you* want to put her in your room?"

"Absolutely not," Chas insisted angrily, and though all of Lily's nerve endings began to crackle with indignation, Chas's older brother burst out laughing.

"You're afraid of her."

Chapter Two

Chas pushed Grant out of the kitchen and into the foyer, not sure how much of their conversation could be heard by the woman in the maid's quarters, and unwilling to take any chances.

"I am not."

"Of course you are!" Grant insisted, laughing. "Look at you, you're all but shaking in your shoes."

"That's ridiculous," Chas said, and strode past his brother toward the den. "Why the hell would I be afraid of a five-foot, ten-inch woman?"

"I don't know," Grant admitted, following closely on Chas's heels. "Let's see. Why would you be afraid of her? Could it be because you find her irresistibly attractive?"

"No woman is irresistibly attractive," Chas said, focusing his attention on straightening up the desk to get ready for his discussion with Lily about salary. To his horror, Grant burst out laughing again.

"Oh, Chas. Who do you think you're talking to here?

I know firsthand that you're more susceptible than the rest of us to a pretty girl. But this time you're not alone. All of us are like putty around someone as gorgeous as Lily.''

Chas pinned him with a look. "Then I guess I don't have anything to worry about, since you've just admitted you find her attractive, too.''

"Of course I do,'' Grant acknowledged with a hearty laugh, then he leaned over the mahogany desk and smiled cunningly. "But I'm not going to be the one alone with her tomorrow night.''

After dinner the following evening, Chas understood exactly what Grant meant. His brother didn't even have to allude to the other mistakes Chas had made in his life. This situation had enough trouble of its own. With the kids fed and happy, the house was unusually quiet. The sun had begun to set, and sporadic lamps made cozy yellow arches of light and cast odd shadows.

All in all the whole place was too intimate.

He paced the living room, knowing he should go up to the nursery and start bathtime, but feeling it was far too dangerous. He convinced himself that Lily could handle the job alone, since Grant had taught her last night to bathe one child at a time while keeping the others entertained in the play yard.

Sighing, Chas sat on the worn office chair and leaned back. In a good many ways he was glad he'd been wrong about Lily. Like Evan's wife, Claire, she certainly had a way with babies. Though Claire had gotten her experience by helping with her younger siblings, Lily hadn't volunteered where she'd garnered her information about raising kids except for her one statement about baby-sitting for her sister. Chas hadn't asked her to elaborate on the situation, though he supposed he should have since that would have been a normal question to ask on an interview...if his brother had let him interview her. But, now that she was here and working, if he asked for details, his probing could be construed as interest in her personal life, and Chas didn't want Lily to think he was interested in her personal life.

Because he wasn't. He really wasn't in the market for a wife. If anything, a casual relationship was about as high on his agenda as a woman could get until his law practice was established and he had a better handle on being Annie's guardian. Since Lily worked for him, a relationship with her was completely out of the question.

So that meant everything had to be aboveboard. Nothing personal between them. She was his employee. He was her boss. And that was that.

Oddly enough, Chas suddenly felt better, maybe more in control. Satisfied that he'd resolved this whole issue in his mind, he rose from his seat. He supposed he could help Lily after all.

Exactly as she had been instructed to do, she'd placed Cody and Taylor in the play yard. When Chas walked into the nursery, he immediately pulled Cody out of the colorful pen and stepped into the bathroom where Lily was bathing Annie.

"Hey, pumpkin," he said, bending to tickle Annie's chin. "You like the water, don't you?"

Annie rewarded him with two swift splashes.

"She certainly is a water baby," Lily agreed, reaching behind her for the towel she'd strategically placed so she wouldn't have to leave Annie's side.

Though Lily wasn't struggling, Chas slid Cody to the floor, pulled Annie from the tub and placed her in the towel Lily held.

"Thanks."

"You're welcome. Anything I can do to help?"

Lily pointed to Cody with her chin. "How about undressing that one for his bath while I dress this one?"

"Sounds good to me," Chas agreed, but as if Cody understood what had been said, he crawled around Chas's legs and out of the room. Chas turned and tried to grab him, but he missed Cody's T-shirt by a millimeter, and the little boy zipped off, giggling.

"Oh, great! We'll be lucky to catch him now. He might only be crawling, but he's a slick one."

"I'm sorry."

"It wasn't your fault. It was mine. I should have known better than to talk so openly about his *b-a-t-h* in front of him."

Lily grinned. "Doesn't like the water?"

Chas thought a second. "Actually, I don't think that's it. I think Cody's just stubborn, like my brother Grant."

As he dashed out of the bathroom after Cody, a perverse part of Chas knew he'd added the afterthought because he didn't like the idea of Grant being attracted to Lily. It hit him that he was jealous of his brother being attracted to a woman neither one of them could have, and he almost groaned. No! No! He couldn't have lost his control this easily...and without warning. For Pete's sake, he'd hardly looked at the woman!

He found Cody cooing to Taylor through the mesh of the play yard and scooped him up. "You're a bad boy today."

Cody giggled, playfully slapped Chas's cheek and said, "Baboy."

Though he knew the child didn't understand what he'd said, Chas sighed. "You won't get any argument out of me." He swung Cody up to the changing table and began removing his clothes. When Cody remembered he'd been running because it was bathtime, he let out a high-pitched squeal.

"Shush!" Chas scolded softly. "Do you want the women to think you're a coward?"

Cody stopped squealing and blinked up at his brother.

"Worse," Chas said, not sure why his little impromptu heart-to-heart talk had caught his brother's interest, but mightily glad that it had. "You're making *me* look bad. Which means you're making both of us look bad."

Cody only peered at him skeptically.

"Trust me, Cody, most of the things you do in life you'll be doing to please a woman...."

"What are you telling that poor, innocent child?"

Caught, Chas felt all the blood drain from his face, but when he peeked behind him and saw Lily smiling, he concluded she hadn't heard enough of his conversation to grasp the real meaning, and he shrugged carelessly.

"I decided it's never too early to start him on the facts of life."

"Then at least tell him both sides of the story," Lily said. After lifting naked Cody off the changing table, she nuzzled his cheek with her nose, then in her most earnest voice said, "Women do a hundred more things to please men than men would even think to do for women. We ask for a few basics like cleanliness," she said, indicating the bathroom to the little boy who looked at her as if he really was trying to understand. "And honesty. Everything else is a matter of personal opinion."

Chas actually thought about that, wondering if she meant what she'd said. *He* could be clean. He could certainly be honest. It would be the easiest relationship of his life....

Lord, what was he doing? Daydreaming about a relationship with her again? This was crazy. Sure, the woman was pretty, and she seemed to be easygoing and nice. But for the love of Heaven, he'd only met her yesterday. He didn't even know her...and, more important, he didn't want a relationship. He'd already had three that were the absolute pits. Besides, he had things to do...

Like get his sister ready for her bath, Chas thought, pulling himself out of his reverie. Then they could put the kids to bed and get into separate rooms before he drove himself crazy.

Chas saw to it that bathing the kids was accomplished quickly. He said good-night to each of the babies and tiptoed out of the room, leaving Lily to wait for the children to fall asleep.

Glad to be alone, he went to the den and opened a bottle of scotch and a file for a case sent to him by a large Philadelphia firm that had agreed to employ him long-distance for research and document writing. Since he needed sustenance until his own practice took off and since he knew nobody could ever have too much experience, Chas was more than willing to take on the low-level job.

"Excuse me, Mr. Brewster...Chas?" Lily said, sheepishly stepping into the den.

Flustered by her unexpected presence, Chas bounced out of his seat. "What's wrong? Is something wrong with one of the kids?"

"No, no," she said, laughing a little and batting her hand in dismissal. "They're all asleep."

"Oh." Chas sat again. "So, what can I do for you?"

"Well, you said we'd discuss my salary and your expectations for me last night, but we never got around to it."

He remembered. After she'd gotten settled, Grant announced that it was bathtime and that *he* would show Lily what to do. Together they'd gone to the nursery, and though Chas had determinedly stayed away, laughter had floated down to him until he rushed upstairs to chaperon.

Chas scowled at the memory.

"I'm sorry," Lily said, obviously responding to the expression on his face. "If this is a bad time, I can come back."

"No. This is a good time," Chas said, putting the bottle of scotch back in the drawer. He was thirty years old and starting his own law practice. Three bad relationships had taught him several good lessons—lessons a man couldn't toss aside for a pretty face. And over a year had passed since the last one. He'd finished law school, paid most of his debts, and kept himself out of trouble the entire time. If he couldn't get a hold of himself long enough to have a conversation with the woman who was caring for the triplets, then he needed his head examined.

"In fact, I should apologize for not remembering to talk with you last night."

"That's okay," she said, meekly making her way into the office. She took the seat on the chair in front of his desk, while Chas organized his thoughts, jotting down a few things on paper so he wouldn't forget them.

As he calmly explained her salary and the Brewster expectations, Chas felt another stab of attraction, but he controlled it by reminding himself of the valuable lesson that he learned with Charlene—good looks were only *part* of the package. Absorbing that, really taking in the full meaning of that lesson, he realized this conversation could actually work to his benefit because he could use it to strengthen his resolve.

Sitting across the desk from him, wearing jeans and a sweatshirt, Lily Andersen was still more attractive than most women dressed for an evening on the town. Her sunny blond hair had been pulled into a loose knot at her nape and pointed out how beautiful, how perfect her face was. High cheekbones, bright with color, accented her large blue eyes. Even unpainted, her pink lips were full, generous. If this were any other place, any other situation, he probably would roll the dice one more time and try for a relationship with her. But because she was his employee and this was his house, having a relationship with her was out of the question. Since his libido couldn't seem to understand that, Chas decided to try to get it under control by reminding himself that looks were frequently deceiving. In the past Chas had made the three biggest mistakes of his life after leaping into relationships with pretty girls, without first gathering enough information about them.

It was time to cure his libido of this affliction once and for all.

"So, Lily, I didn't really get a chance to interview you yesterday, and there are still a few questions I'd like to ask you."

She smiled. Her face lit with pleasure. Her blue eyes sparkled.

Chas's libido went on red alert. There was no way a man could find anything wrong with that face...with that smile.

"Like what?"

Chas cleared his throat, telling his libido to cool its

heels for a few seconds and he'd find a flaw, a reason not to like her. "Well, you talked about caring for your sister's children, but I was curious about other child-care experience you'd had."

"None, really," Lily answered easily, truthfully.

Chas waited for her to elaborate, but she didn't. She sat with her hands on her lap, her soft smile firmly in place and her blue eyes clear and direct.

Chas's libido laughed. She was honest and unpretentious. She didn't try to fake or fudge her résumé. She was quite definitely a take-me-as-I-am person. No pretense or artifice here. Strike one on trying to make her unattractive.

"College?"

She shook her head. "I'm afraid not. I never wanted to go to college, I only wanted to get married and have a family."

Chas mentally snickered at his libido.

"Really?" he said, getting comfortable in his chair, thinking he was finally on the road to proving his point. There was nothing more unattractive than a woman who needed a man to complete herself.

"Really," Lily said, and gave Chas another pretty smile. "Frankly," she said with a self-deprecating sigh. "I fell in love in high school. Everett was good-looking, smart and loved his family. He was *everything* a woman could possibly want in a man. I was so enamored I couldn't see straight. I would have sacrificed anything for him."

Chas's libido didn't say a word. It didn't have to. Only a fool would have missed the sincerity in her explanation. She hadn't needed a man to complete herself, she'd fallen in love. And she'd been loyal and trustworthy. If only one of his women had been loyal or trustworthy....

Strike two.

"So what happened?" Chas asked quietly.

"I waited for him while he went to college, forgave a couple of indiscretions, then suffered public humiliation when he left me at the altar a couple of weeks ago—white dress, bridesmaids, impatient minister and all."

Chas and his libido tried to picture it and couldn't. It didn't make any sense that a normal, red-blooded man would leave this beautiful, charming, sweet, sincere woman at the altar. The man must have been an absolute fool.

"I'm sorry. What did you say?"

Chas didn't realize he'd spoken aloud, but deduced he must have mumbled or she wouldn't have needed a repeat. "I said that was absolutely cruel."

"It was cruel," Lily agreed softly. "And painful."

"And that's why you left Wisconsin," Chas said, finishing her thought for her. It all made perfect sense to him now. A beautiful woman shows up on his doorstep with no purpose or direction in life, save that of wanting to help him with his kids. He should have known. She was rebounding from another relationship.

Even as Chas breathed a sigh of relief because he knew only a blockhead got involved with someone who had two weeks ago been publicly jilted, his libido didn't seem to have any problem with her story at all.

Though he judged himself to be an honest, honorable man who would never take advantage of a struggling, vulnerable woman, he also knew he'd lost this battle, because his intellect and integrity weren't the problem. His libido was.

Chapter Three

A beam of bright autumn sunshine woke Lily. Slowly, contentedly, she opened her eyes to the golden warmth.

As she stretched languidly, like a cat stirring from a nap on a sunny sidewalk, she recognized she was happy for the first time in weeks. She knew it was because she'd finally found a job. Then she suddenly realized that she should have been awakened in the middle of the night to help care for the triplets, and she should probably be feeding them breakfast right now.

Bouncing out of bed, she glanced at the clock and groaned. Nine-thirty! She was late. She couldn't afford to be irresponsible. She needed this job too much. She had less than fifty dollars to her name, and not only did staying employed mean she had a source for a paycheck for an undetermined span of time, it also meant she was going to be fed and housed courtesy of Grant and Chas Brewster.

The very thought of Chas stopped Lily dead in her tracks. She remembered his lean, athletic body and the sensual grace with which he moved. She remembered his shrewd, assessing gray-green eyes. She remembered his thick, sandy brown hair.

Unfortunately she was directly in front of the mirror and saw that her own hair was going in every direction, she wasn't wearing a stitch of makeup, and her one-piece flannel pajamas were covered with skiing bears.

Confused, she blinked twice, waiting for her mind to refocus. Surely she didn't care what she looked like. Because if she did, it could only mean that she cared what Chas Brewster thought of her. And she didn't care what he thought of her...did she?

No, she couldn't. Could she?

No. Absolutely not, she decided, drawing in a long, life-sustaining breath of air. For Pete's sake, falling too hard for a man was what had gotten her into this predicament in the first place. She couldn't even *look* at another man until she got her life straightened out.

Nonetheless, she needed to hide the bears.

Grabbing a robe from the chair on her way to the door, Lily hurried out of her bedroom. She put the robe on while still standing in the alcove, then entered the kitchen, yanking the drawstring belt.

"I'm sorry," she said before she even said good-morning.

"That's quite all right," Chas said politely, scooping a bit of oatmeal from Annie's chin and rerouting it to her mouth.

Before she could stop herself, Lily noticed how relaxed and sexy he looked in his jeans and sweatshirt. She also noted that although his haircut was neat, certain strands tumbled boyishly over his forehead. Unfortunately she simultaneously realized that she was paying attention to how handsome he was—again! Why was it she couldn't be in the same room with him without this awareness of him?

"Everybody's first day with the triplets is hard," he said, still not looking at her. "I thought I'd cut you a break and let you sleep in today."

"Because I'm going to be the one getting up with the kids tonight?" Lily speculated, walking to the coffee-maker on the counter beside the sink, telling herself to ignore her attraction to him. She was a mere two weeks out of a six-year relationship. It was too soon to think she was finding another man attractive—even though he was. In fact, that was probably the point. Chas Brewster was a commanding, regal, masculine man. He probably attracted women the same way cheesecake attracted dieters.

She found a cup and poured coffee into it, forcing her mind off Chas and on to her surroundings. The entire kitchen was immaculately white, as was a good bit of the rest of the house. From that alone, Lily surmised the place had been decorated before the triplets were born. She didn't have a clue how the father of three grown men could end up with three infants, but she figured that wasn't her business. When the Brewsters were ready, they would tell her the story behind their father and stepmother. If they never told her, she would consider herself lucky to be able to avoid village gossip.

"No, you won't be handling the kids tonight. I can do it myself," Chas said agreeably. "Mostly they sleep through the night, anyway, and if they don't, I know how to keep them occupied until I can get each one fed, diapered or rocked."

"But you're not supposed to care for the kids alone," Lily protested, realizing that not only were Taylor and Cody happily chewing on play toys, but all three babies were dressed. He hadn't sought her help with the kids in the night. He'd taken care of morning detail. Now he was planning to assume night duty again. "I *want* to help you."

"And you will," Chas said, still agreeable, still concentrating on Annie. "I have a meeting in town in about an hour and a half. Once I get through here, they're all yours."

"This isn't what I was hired to do," Lily argued, fearing for her job now that Grant was gone. She'd completely forgotten Chas hadn't wanted to hire her; Grant had. But Grant wasn't here and Chas was acting as though he didn't need her. This time tomorrow she could be back on the street. "We're supposed to be working together."

"We don't have to work together," Chas said breezily, but he stopped the spoon on its way to Annie's mouth as if he'd suddenly thought of something. "Unless you don't think you can handle the kids by yourself," he said, finally turning to look at her.

Lily felt as if time had come to a screeching halt. Looking confused and shocked, he peered at her hair, her face, and the bear-covered pajama leg that peeked out from beneath the hem of her pink chenille robe. A noise sounding like a groan or a laugh erupted from the back of his throat, but before Lily could be sure, he brought his hand to his mouth and pretended to cough.

"You *can* manage the kids alone, can't you?" he asked slowly, his voice shaking as if he were desperately trying to control it.

She suspected he was laughing at her, and her chin lifted. "Why don't you just go and get ready for your meeting...or change clothes or brief yourself on your notes. I'll take care of the kids."

"No," he said, then coughed to clear his throat again. "That's fine. *I'm* fine. Why don't you go shower or whatever and I'll finish up here?"

"Because we're supposed to be working together," Lily insisted, determined to make her point. She didn't care if he didn't like her hair, her lack of makeup or her pajamas. She wasn't losing this job without a fight. "What do the kids usually do now?" she asked, walking to Taylor's high chair. Seeing that Chas had dressed all three babies in little sweatpants, T-shirts and tiny tennis shoes, she said, "If they're going outside, I can take them outside. If they usually watch 'Sesame Street,' I can take them to the family room. I'm perfectly qualified."

"You're also in your pajamas," Chas said, sounding exasperated. "You can't go outside."

Lily glanced down at her robe. "I could still take them into the family room to watch TV," she mumbled indignantly.

"Or you could take your shower and really be ready to care for them when I leave."

Lily saw she was being foolish and combed her fingers through her unruly hair. "Sorry."

"That's okay," Chas said patiently. "Working with the triplets takes a while to get used to."

"That's not it," Lily said, deciding she had to get this out in the open or she'd make herself crazy. It was hard enough to deal privately with her attraction to him. She couldn't handle worrying about being fired, too. "I'm afraid you're going to fire me, and I can't afford to lose this job."

Chas busied himself with Annie again. "I'm not going to fire you."

Though it wasn't a sweeping declaration of competency, Lily recognized that it had to be enough. She was justifiably insecure, because her ego had taken a real beating when Everett had left her at the altar. But more than that, she knew if she didn't soon trust someone about something, she'd never reenter the real world. Chas might not be promising her a job forever, but he was backhandedly telling her he felt she was qualified to care for his three children, and that was a big, important deal. Knowing how much he and his brother Grant adored these kids, she understood they wouldn't trust them to just anyone.

She nodded. "Okay. Then I'll stop driving you nuts. I'll shower and get dressed, and everything will go back to normal."

Long after she was gone, Chas continued to stare at the alcove. He stared so long that it took two squeals from Annie before he came back to the present. He wasn't an idiot. He knew that Lily would have some self-doubt from being left at the altar. Anybody would. But he still found her last statement incomprehensible. How could anyone as absolutely stunning as she was— a woman who brought him to groaning despair even without makeup, with sleep-tousled hair, and wearing pajamas covered with bears—ever think any house in which she lived would be normal?

Chas left the house about two hours later but not without making a big production about saying goodbye, leaving telephone numbers and giving Lily so many instructions she knew there was no way she could remember them all.

Particularly when she was having such a hard time concentrating on what he was saying.

It hadn't occurred to her that he would have to dress for a business meeting, and when he walked down the spiral staircase, looking like someone off the cover of *GQ* she almost fainted. But it was the way he kissed each child goodbye, giving them individualized words of affection to make each one feel special, that really snagged her heart.

Before it was all over she could have hugged him for being so charmingly sweet to those babies. But thinking about hugging him tumbled into thinking about kissing him, and the mere thought of his lips touching hers sent a bubble of excitement through her, and she couldn't get him out of the house fast enough.

When the sound of his car finally faded into silence, she breathed a sigh of relief.

"What is the matter with me? How could I get flustered so easily?" she asked the three eight-month-old babies who sat in the play yard staring up at her. "You'd swear I'd never seen a man in a suit before," she added, bending to pick up a spongy ball, that had been tossed over the net railing by one of the kids, though none of them had cried or squealed for it.

She was glad they were happily settled, because she needed a minute to deliberate on this. In spite of what she'd told the kids, she understood that the problem wasn't merely that Chas was physically attractive—though that masked the real culprit. The truth was, in a matter of two days Chas Brewster had begun to endear himself to her because he was so loving with the children.

She confirmed that conclusion when Chas returned home that afternoon and barely put down his briefcase before he reached into the play yard, stroking Cody's hair, as he scooped Annie out and cooed to Taylor.

Leaning against the den door, Lily smiled, confident that she would be able to keep herself in line, now that

she had deduced she was losing control because he was
a sweetheart with the triplets. Any woman would be
charmed by a man who could be so genuinely good to
kids.

Grateful that her attraction wasn't unusual, she gladly
deemed this particular dilemma to be manageable. But
when Chas turned and pierced her with a look, one of
those uniquely masculine expressions that turns most
women's knees to jelly, Lily felt as if her stomach had
fallen to the floor. She decided that for every bit as adorable as he was around the kids, and for every bit as much
as she believed that was the bottom line to her attraction,
she couldn't discount the fact that he was a virile, sexy
man.

"You didn't have any problems while I was gone, did
you?"

"No. Everything was fine."

He couldn't have hidden his relief if he'd tried.
"Good. Thank God."

Lily ventured into the room. "Mr. Brewster, I'm actually very competent with children."

"Please don't call me, Mr. Brewster," Chas said,
walking away from her, Annie on his arm. "You make
me feel like my father."

"I'm sorry," Lily said. He was doing it again. Avoid-
ing her at all costs. He didn't want her help at breakfast,
now it appeared he didn't even want to talk with her.
She wondered if it was because she was obvious in her
attraction for him, and felt the heat of embarrassment
rising to her cheeks. "I'll try to remember to call you
Chas, but to be honest, I'm a little awkward with that."

He turned, faced her. "Why?" he asked curiously.

"Well, you're my boss, and I've always suspected

that when a person had a boss, they should be respectful.''

"You are respectful," Chas mumbled and again
turned away from her, balancing Annie on one arm while
he yanked his tie off with the other. "I don't need to be
called mister or sir or any of that nonsense. If we're
going to be living together, Lily, we're going to have to
get accustomed to each other.''

For the first time since she'd met him, Lily realized
that getting accustomed to each other was probably going to be as hard for him as it would be for her. As long
as everything was clear-cut and professional, he was all
right with her, capable of doing whatever needed to be
done. But the minute things turned personal, as they frequently did since they were living in the same house, he
got quiet, evasive. He never seemed to want to be in the
same room with her, didn't like sharing the chores. Because she'd been wrapped up in her own reaction to him,
Lily hadn't seen he was reacting every bit as poorly to
her.

She remembered again that he hadn't wanted to hire
her and that he'd had the typical initial male response to
her. He either thought she was a bubble brain or riffraff,
though she hadn't yet figured out which one. She considered being angry, considered letting him deal with the
problem himself, but didn't want to live with anyone
who had such a terrible impression of her. As a part of
the stronger, more powerful person she needed to become, she chose to change his opinion of her.

"I don't think it will be so difficult to get accustomed
to each other," she said brightly. "First off we share a
very important bond.''

When he faced her he looked pained, as if sharing a
bond with her hurt him somehow. "And what is that?''

"Well, we both love the kids," Lily said carefully, praying she didn't make things worse by being so bold. "I know I've just been around them two days. But it would be impossible not to love such beautiful babies."

Chas smiled. "They are beautiful."

"And well behaved," Lily added hopefully, recognizing she had struck a cord and was making progress. "You and your brothers can be very proud of the good job you've done with them so far."

"We've only had them three months," Chas said with a self-deprecating grin that was so endearing and cute, Lily could have happily melted at his feet, but she didn't because she had a mission to accomplish. She had to make this man like her, and she had to do it quickly before he lost patience and got rid of her.

Seeing small talk was working, she walked a few steps closer to the desk. "Your father and stepmother were killed in an accident, right?"

He nodded. "Yeah. It was a shock."

"But at least you all had each other. It's not like the babies went to strangers."

"Actually, they did," Chas said, taking the seat behind the desk and settling Annie on his lap. "My brothers and I had been estranged from our father. We hadn't even been told about the triplets."

"Oh," Lily said, not knowing what else to say and not really wanting to probe, because they'd passed the boundaries of need-to-know information. Though she was anxious to help Chas grow comfortable with her, she knew what it was like to have people asking questions she didn't want to answer—questions she sometimes couldn't answer—and she refused to pry for information that wasn't any of her business.

"It's okay," Chas said. "You're going to hear the

gossip in town, anyway. I might as well tell you the story before you hear various and sundry versions that are a little more colorful than they need to be.''

"All right," Lily said, seeing that he meant what he said and understanding his reasoning. Usually gossip was far, far worse than the truth. He motioned for her to sit as he gathered his thoughts, and she took a seat on the chair in front of the huge mahogany desk.

For several seconds Chas didn't say anything, and when he did speak it was softly. "My mother died suddenly. She had a heart attack, and the doctor said she went so quickly nothing could have been done for her."

"I'm sorry."

Chas nodded his acceptance of her condolence. "It was pretty bad. We all took it very hard. Grant was the worst. He drank himself silly and in general made a nuisance of himself in town. We were all so concerned about him that we hardly paid any attention to my father. The only thing I can clearly remember him saying was that life was short, and he felt he had wasted his."

"That's a fairly normal reaction," Lily confirmed gently, leaning forward, listening to him.

Chas drew in a long breath, awkwardly aware of how good it felt to discuss the situation openly and objectively with someone. He hadn't realized how much he'd needed to talk about this, and he suspected part of the reason everything seemed to want to tumble out of him was because he didn't know Lily. She had no preconceived notions and didn't seem judgmental. He also didn't have to worry that things he said would come back to haunt him two years from now, because two years from now she might not be here. Whatever the reason for being able to talk to her, he was just glad to have the opportunity to get some of this off his chest.

"In our own grief," Chas said, though he knew he was rationalizing, "we more or less ignored Dad. One day he came home with a spectacular-looking woman. A tall redhead with sad brown eyes. And we all suspected that he was going to try to set her up with Grant."

"But he had married her," Lily put in quietly when Chas fell silent.

He nodded.

"And they had the triplets...."

"No, we had a big fight, raised hell in the local bars for about a week, then stormed out of town as if we had every right to punish Dad."

"Are you sure you didn't?"

Chas smiled somberly when she seemingly took his side. "We'll never know. We didn't stay around long enough to hear the whole story. My brothers and I got together in Philadelphia, where I was going to school, and made a pact that none of us would ever go home. After a week or so, Grant ran into a family friend who had left Brewster County a few years before. Hunter had started a construction company but he had too much work and couldn't handle it all, so Grant threw in his lot with him and moved to Georgia. Evan took his life savings and invested it in a company that buys and manages fast-food franchises. Because his entire future was on the line, Evan poured his heart and soul and all his time into that company."

"And you?"

"And I made a mess of my life."

"But you were already in law school."

"Yeah," Chas said, but in such a self-condemning tone he knew he had to explain himself. "Unfortunately, I also got married twice, divorced twice, was thrown in jail because my wife wrote bad checks and nearly went bankrupt.''

"You did all that in two years?''

"A little over one year. I work fast.''

Lily couldn't help it, she laughed. "I'll say you do. You make me feel lazy and slow for only having one relationship in six years.''

"Consider yourself lucky and smart for only having one relationship in six years.''

Lily sighed heavily. "I do, some days. Other days I just feel like an idiot because I didn't see that Everett had completely lost interest.''

"You think that's what happened?'' Chas asked skeptically.

She shrugged. "I don't know. All I know is that one day I was planning to spend the rest of my life with the man I loved and the next I was alone and didn't have a future.''

"Trust me,'' Chas said. "You're better off.''

"You think so?''

"I *know* so. You don't want to be in a relationship with someone who isn't committed. I've been there and done that.'' He shook his head.

Lily giggled.

"I've felt stupid, looked stupid and gone broke because of it,'' Chas said, then he laughed. He laughed long and hard, for the first time seeing the humor in it. "I must have seemed like a real dope to the rest of the world,'' he said, then suddenly he stopped laughing and looked at Lily. "Oh, I'll bet my brothers thought I was absolutely crazy.''

"Or distraught,'' Lily suggested kindly.

He grabbed her rationale like a drowning man grabs a life preserver. "Really?''

"Sure," Lily said encouragingly. "For heaven's sake, you'd lost your mother, then your father. You left your home, but your brothers deserted you. You were looking for company, companionship, maybe even a sense of the future. You weren't crazy. You weren't even so much lonely as you probably were grasping at straws."

Juggling Annie on his lap, Chas considered that. "I spent most of the time I was away trying to figure out where I'd be twenty years from now. I wanted a plan. No, what I really wanted was a crystal ball. I wanted someone to show me that everything was going to turn out okay. And nobody could."

Lily stayed silent for so long that eventually Chas glanced at her. He understood that she'd waited until she had his attention before she very gently said, "Nobody can. And nobody ever will."

"I know," he said. But after she'd left the room, Chas leaned back on his father's old office chair and sighed. He wondered if she would be so sweet to him if she knew he wanted nothing more than to sleep with her. He'd deliberately told his story to the bitter end, because in a sense that's truly what it was. A bitter end. He would never marry again. Not because he didn't want all the things he believed marriage offered, and not because he was too busy setting up his practice, but because he absolutely refused to be a three-time loser. The first time he'd married and divorced he blamed fate and stupidity for his mistake, but the second he hadn't been quite the idiot he let his brothers believe. He'd loved Charlene. She'd loved him. In the end love wasn't enough. He would never trust it again, so he would never fall again. It was that simple.

So he had indirectly warned Lily and hoped she was smart enough to heed his admonition, because now that

he knew she was as sweet as she was beautiful, he
wasn't exactly sure how much longer he was going to
be able to hide his attraction to her.

Though Lily hadn't wanted it to, Chas's explanation
of his past had made him more attractive because it
showed he was a sensitive, honest man. But, thankfully,
it also opened her mind to all kinds of new vantage
points on the situation.

With him busy doing legal research, Lily had a whole
afternoon to remind herself that they lived in the same
house, in a small town, where he was trying to establish
himself as a lawyer. After some of the mistakes he made,
he didn't need to be the victim of any more gossip,
which he would be if they somehow got romantically
involved.

Before dinner, she recognized that any relationship
between them would be doomed because they were both
jaded and cautious. She hadn't missed the bitterness in
his voice. Not only that, but *she* was still hurting. There
was nothing like public humiliation for pain and suffering. She felt as if she'd been seared the whole way to
her soul. If Chas's residual pain was half as bad as hers
was, they would never make it together.

By the time bathtime came around, she decided that
she wouldn't have wanted a relationship with him, anyway. She wasn't injured enough to believe that *all* men
were scum, but a smart woman would have to question
how one man could get married and divorced from two
women in a little over one year. And she was a smart
woman. The common denominator in his bad relationships was him. If he thought she was a bubble brain or
a bad apple, he should see what she was beginning to
think about him.

Later that night when she was rocking Taylor to sleep, Chas joined her in the nursery. "Isn't she beautiful?" he whispered, sliding his fingers across the jagged row of feathery hair on her forehead.

Wary, but also recognizing her place as an employee, Lily diplomatically said, "Yes. All three of the kids are beautiful."

"And so different," Chas said, still watching the little girl. "It never ceases to amaze me that God goes to so much effort to make each one of us different, and then we go to an equal amount of effort trying to be the same."

Remembering trends and fashions and haircuts and hair colors she'd tried in high school when she was desperate to fit in, Lily laughed and said, "I never thought of that."

"That's because you were probably the person everybody was trying to copy."

He said it with such sincerity that he shocked Lily, and she glanced up at him. From the way he looked at her, she knew he didn't see her high school struggles, or even a woman rejected at the altar. And he definitely didn't see a dumb blonde. She wasn't sure what he saw, but whatever it was, it was good. Better, even, than how she saw herself. Their eyes locked, and a strong force of energy arced between them. Try as she might she couldn't pull her gaze away.

She reminded herself of his two marriages in one year, and that the breakups could very well have been his fault. She recalled that he was jaded and bitter and probably wouldn't marry again. Then she remembered that *she* was jaded and bitter and shouldn't even be looking at a man until she got herself together over the one who dumped her. But none of that helped in the face of the current that crackled between them.

"She's asleep now. You can put her to bed."

Lily licked her dry lips, unwilling to release his gaze. She'd never been so confused in her life. In all their dealings, she always felt him pulling away from her or warning her off as he'd done with his stories that afternoon. She'd believed that was because of his initial reaction to her, but right at this minute he seemed helplessly drawn to her.

Now, that was truly grasping at straws, Lily thought, mentally reprimanding herself for being foolishly vain. Perceiving herself a failure because of Everett's desertion, she was falling for the first man to come along. And she was also endowing him with feelings for her that he couldn't possibly have in such a short period of time.

In other words, she was rebounding.

The sense of relief she felt when she had that thought was nearly overwhelming. This time when she stared into Chas's fathomless green eyes, she told herself the jolt she got was the result of *wanting* to feel something. So it was merely a figment of her imagination.

"I'll put her in her crib soon," she said. "Right now, if you don't mind, I'd like a minute to rock her."

She smiled when he nodded his acceptance and tiptoed out of the room, but when he was gone, Lily sagged in the rocking chair.

His eyes were full of wisdom, full of pain. Add those soulful eyes to a strong-boned face and a body most men got only with sweat and sacrifice at the gym, and Lily was hard-pressed to remember her name, let alone that all the emotion churning through her was something she created to ease the pain of her rejection.

She'd never realized rebounding could feel so much better, so much stronger than real sexual attraction, because she'd never felt anything even remotely this powerful for Everett.

The worst of it was, she knew she had to figure out a way to control this fascination she had with her new employer, because if she didn't she was absolutely certain it had every intention of controlling her.

And until she proved herself to these people, she didn't dare make one false move. In fact, what she should be doing is pulling out all the stops to make them believe they couldn't live without her.

Chapter Four

"Hello, is anybody home?"

When Lily heard the call of the soft, melodious voice, she dropped the towel she was folding and ran to the foyer. Not only were the babies asleep, but Chas was busy researching a legal brief and Grant was in the den, studying a request for bids, and she didn't want them disturbed.

As far as Lily was concerned, all was right with the world.

If it killed her, she planned to keep it that way.

She stepped into the foyer, where a beautiful dark-haired woman and an equally attractive sandy-haired man stood grinning at her.

"Can I help you?" she asked carefully.

"I'm Evan Brewster and this is my wife, Claire," the man said, extending his hand to her as he made the introduction.

She took it. "It's nice to meet you, Mr. Brewster. I'm Lily," she said, "the kids' new nanny."

"Oh," Evan said, obviously surprised. "I thought you were…"

"She's the nanny," Chas emphatically stated, walking up the hall from the den. "The *nanny*."

"All right, she's the nanny," Evan said, conceding the issue. "Where are the kids?"

"Sleeping," Lily said, lowering her voice to a whisper. "But I've got some peanut butter cookies and a fresh pot of coffee in the kitchen to keep you busy until they wake up."

Grant poked his head out of the study. "Peanut butter cookies?" he asked, almost drooling.

"Yes, and they're very good," Lily said, leading Evan Brewster, his wife and a reluctant Chas back to the kitchen. "They're sort of my specialty."

"And they're sort of my favorite," Grant said, edging his way through the crowd to walk beside her. "Do you make them soft or crunchy?"

"I can do both."

"I love you," Grant said, squeezing his eyes shut with ecstasy.

Lily laughed. "That's what they all say," she joked, presenting her employers with a plate of soft, warm cookies. "Anyone for coffee?"

After a general round of agreement, Lily watched as everyone took a cookie or two and meandered to the round table in the semicircle of windows which served as a breakfast nook.

A syrupy, tingly delight enveloped her as she poured coffee and provided the group with a bowl of sugar and pitcher of cream. This was more like what she expected this job to be. Not only was she doing the work, but she was on friendly, happy terms with everyone. She wasn't merely blending in, the transitions were seamless, effortless, as if the Brewsters, too, believed this was the way things should be. And the more they got accustomed to letting her take over the routine chores, the greater the possibility she'd soon be indispensable.

"Evan and Claire were in New York for their honeymoon," Grant said, including Lily in the conversation with his explanation. "You should come over and listen so they only have to tell their stories once."

"There aren't any stories to tell," Evan said, but he laughed. "We spent most of our time in jewelry stores."

"You promised me a really nice diamond if I married you," Claire said. "All I did was hold you to that promise."

"Can I see it?" Lily asked, happily curious, though she would have thought viewing another woman's engagement or wedding rings might have been difficult. Instead, when Claire extended her left hand and displayed the three-carat marquis diamond flanked by two rubies, a wonderful womanly sense of joy filled her and she gasped with delight. "It's spectacular."

"Men have no taste. Always pick out your own ring," Claire teased, but she turned and dropped a quick kiss on her husband's lips.

Lily expected a reaction to that, as well. This time she had to admit there was a twinge. Not jealousy, but loss. Right about now she would have been returning from her honeymoon, too, because unlike Evan and Claire, who only had a week, she and Everett had planned almost a month in Aruba.

"These are great cookies," Grant said, interrupting her thoughts.

"Terrific cookies," Claire agreed, eyeing Lily closely as though she could see something was wrong.

Realizing some of what she'd been thinking must

have registered in her expression, and at least two of the Brewsters felt sorry for her, Lily busied herself with re-filling the cookie dish. "Thank you. I love to bake," she said. "You should see what I do at Christmastime. I bake, paint, sprinkle and decorate until I have enough cookies for an army."

"I'm expecting you to be here at Christmastime," Grant said emphatically.

Lily laughed, relaxing again, but Chas scowled. He was thinking that *he* should have done what Grant did. He should have jumped in and saved Lily when she started having painful thoughts about her crumbled re-lationship. Grant, of all people, Mr. Insensitive, had beaten him to the punch.

Taylor's very distinct cry erupted from the monitor behind the table before Chas could put in his two cents' worth or try to make up for missing the obvious.

"Oh, it's Taylor!" Claire cried, and started to rise to get her.

"No, I'll get her," Lily insisted. "She's undoubtedly wet," she said, glancing at Claire's white wool traveling suit. "I promise I'll bring her down the second she's changed."

Claire smiled gratefully, however Grant pushed back his chair and stood up. "I'll come with you."

"No, you stay and visit," Lily said, waving him back down, but he followed anyway.

Chas merely stared at his older brother.

"Lily, you might have only been here a few days," Grant said, as he and Lily went to check on the kids. "But you know how this goes. One kid wakes up and before you get to the nursery to quiet her, she's awak-ened her brother or sister, too."

Deciding not to make a mountain out of a molehill,

because Grant might genuinely be interested in helping with the kids, Chas drew a long breath and turned back to Evan and Claire—both of whom were staring at him.

"What?" he asked, indignant.

Evan shrugged. "She's very pretty."

"No kidding," Chas said, trying to keep the snarl out of his voice. As if he needed to be reminded Lily was pretty.

"I'm just a little curious about how you convinced Grant to hire her."

"Grant insisted we hire her. I was the dissenting vote, but since there were only two of us, the vote was tied, and we compromised. She's here for a trial period."

"Well, I hope her trial period extends beyond the holidays," Claire said, examining her soft peanut butter cookie. "I can hardly wait to see what she'll do with gingerbread or fruit horns."

Before Chas had a chance to react to that, Grant marched into the kitchen holding Taylor. Beaming, Lily walked behind him empty armed.

"It was the strangest thing," Grant said, handing Taylor to Claire, who gasped with pleasure. "Neither Cody nor Annie even stirred. They're still sleeping soundly."

"In other words, you really hadn't needed to go upstairs."

Chas couldn't help it, the words were out before he could stop them. Recognizing he'd spoken out of jealousy, both his brothers froze, then gave him an incredulous look.

Chas raised his hands as if conceding defeat. "I'm going back to writing my brief."

"Yeah, you do that," Grant said firmly, but Chas stopped. Basically Grant had just ordered him out of the room, away from Lily. As if it wasn't bad enough that he'd drooled over her cookies, jumped in and comforted her when she was pining over her lost relationship, and then followed her up to the nursery, now he was kicking Chas out of the kitchen.

He didn't like this. Not one damned bit. But there was also nothing he could do without making himself look foolish.

He hoped that was the point Grant was making, but when he saw how close Grant stood to Lily, as the others all cooed over Taylor, Chas didn't really think it was.

Evan and Claire stayed for dinner, and though Claire and Lily volunteered to do the cooking, Grant somehow ended up in the kitchen to keep them company. Chas seethed inside. Here he was, doing his damnedest to control himself around Lily, while Grant followed after her like a lovesick puppy.

And Lily seemed to eat it up.

She smiled at Grant when he pulled out her chair for her, spoke directly to him at times, because it seemed as if he was hanging on her every word, and all but served him a second helping of mashed potatoes when he'd only asked her to pass the bowl.

If all that weren't bad enough, when the meal was completed, Grant helped her with her chair and ushered her upstairs when Claire and Evan went to the nursery to gather clothing for Cody and to kiss the baby girls good-night.

Confused, angry even, Chas went outside for some fresh air, then took a brisk walk.

When he returned, Evan and Claire had gone, taking Cody with them, and Grant had settled down in the study to continue working. Chas began washing the dinner dishes. About the time he had a sinkful of glasses and was up to his elbows in bubbles, Lily walked in.

Seeing him, she stopped dead in her tracks, and Chas mentally sighed. Though he'd warned her about his past failed relationships, he hadn't expected it to cause her to hate him. She could laugh and joke with Evan and Claire and borderline flirt with Grant, but anytime she got near him she froze...just as she had now at the kitchen door.

"You can come in. I don't bite," he said, keeping the anger out of his voice only with great effort.

"I know that," she said slowly as she entered the room with equal care and caution. "And you don't have to do the dishes. That's my job."

"No, it's not," Chas contradicted, annoyed again. "There is no *your* job or *my* job or anybody's job until we get a housekeeper. Then we'll divvy up the chores. Until then, we all have to do a little bit of everything."

"Fine," she said, crossing her arms on her chest. "Then let my little bit be the dishes."

"I've already started the dishes."

"Then what am I supposed to do?"

"Why is it so important that you do something? You've been working since you got up this morning. Why don't you just sit down and relax?"

"Why don't you?"

Because of the confrontational tone of her voice, he looked at her. "I didn't realize we were in competition."

"We're not," Lily said, casually reaching for a dish towel and grabbing a plate to dry. "Not really."

"But you're not going to let me get ahead of you by having me do the dishes by myself, are you?" he asked pointedly, but he grinned stupidly. It was as if they were playing some kind of game and neither of them knew what it was, and neither of them knew the other's rules. It was foolish. Ridiculous. So absurd it was comical.

He watched the great effort it took for her to hide her own smile. "Not on your life."

Chas cupped his hand in the top layer of warm bubbles, scooped some out and flicked them at her. "There. I just threw soap at you. Are you going to top that, or copy it?"

She sniffed daintily. "Neither. I'm going to ignore it."

"Yeah, right," Chas said, laughing. "I know you'll even the score somehow. Why are we competing, anyway?"

"We're not competing."

"Sure we are. Otherwise, you'd be in the family room watching TV right now."

"Just because I don't want to watch television doesn't mean that we're competing."

"No, but helping me with the dishes does, especially since I told you I wanted to do them alone." He let the clock tick off the clock in silence, then, focusing his attention on viciously scrubbing an already-clean plate, he said, "Is our competition what makes you freeze up every time I'm in the room?"

"I don't freeze up," she said, but he noticed she shifted away from him.

"Okay, freeze up or walk away from me."

"I don't," she began, but seemed to recognize that she was about three feet farther away than she'd started out. She sighed heavily.

Chas took advantage of the opportunity to slide toward her, knowing that if she moved she proved his point. When she didn't even attempt to move, he got a little closer. She stiffened a bit, but stayed where she was, so he took the last few steps until he was standing directly in front of her.

Grasping her chin in his soap-bubble-covered fingers, he forced her to look at him and said, "There. Was that so bad?"

"No, but you have an irritating habit of trying to cover me with bubbles."

Without any more provocation than that, he imagined her sitting in the huge oval tub of the master suite, candles scattered throughout the room, sank to her shoulders in frothy suds, a contented smile on her lips. Her eyes would be closed, blocking out the world, and the amber light of the candles would combine with moonlight streaming in through the skylight, making her hair a golden halo and her skin luminescent.

She glanced up at him and the air seemed to sizzle between them. Back in the present, he wondered if maybe the reason she froze when he got near was that she found him as attractive as he found her. That was the theory he wanted to believe, particularly with her plump, inviting mouth only a foot or so away and her eyes large and round with anticipation.

He reasoned that what he ought to do is kiss her. One kiss might actually settle this matter for both of them.

His gaze traveled down to her lips again, then returned to her indigo eyes. He saw questions there, hundreds of them, but he also saw fear and recognized it might be the result of her recent heartbreak, and none of his doing at all. In the silent kitchen he swore he could hear his heart beating wildly in anticipation. But he also knew that if her heart were beating as rapidly, it might not be anticipation or even curiosity. More than likely it would be from panic.

He pulled away.

"All right, since neither one of us wants to clean the

entire kitchen, I'll keep my hands in the sink. You do the drying.''

He clearly heard her breathe a sigh of relief and mentally chastised himself.

"That will work.''

"Good, because I don't want us arguing anymore.''

"Neither do I,'' she admitted quietly.

"Why do we argue?''

"I think because I'm afraid you're going to fire me.''

He glanced at her. "Still?''

She shrugged. "Still.''

"You think it might be a little residual paranoia from your boyfriend recently dumping you?''

"Could be.''

"Well stop thinking about it. Stop worrying about it. Once you've won Grant's heart, you're in. You don't have anything to fear.'' Deciding he wanted to put a little emphasis on that, Chas stopped washing dishes and peered over his shoulder at her. "I mean that,'' he said, referring more to his intention of controlling himself around her than firing her.

She nodded. "Thanks.''

"You're welcome,'' Chas said, trying to sound happy, but he wasn't. It was an aberration for a single man to stifle the sexual urges he had for a single, available, beautiful woman. So even though his mind could understand this whole thing, his libido began to pout.

"While I'm gone, could you please do me a favor and give Claire a call to see if she'll run the ad for the housekeeper one more time?'' Grant asked as he grabbed his garment bag and headed for the front door on his way to Savannah again.

"Actually, I don't have a problem with placing the ad myself. I think I know what we need," Lily said.

"I think you do, too," he agreed happily.

Lily blossomed under his approval. She knew that he was trying to bring her back into the land of the living by praising her and giving her tasks that would boost her sense of confidence, and she appreciated it. After only a little more than a week here, she had very strong familial feelings for the Brewsters. She felt very much like Grant's little sister. And she sensed from his behavior that he fancied himself a big brother to her.

Unfortunately, Chas still scowled at everything Lily did. In spite of their truce, Chas couldn't treat her normally. But the odd part of it was, she preferred when he was scowling at her. Because when he wasn't, he looked at her with such longing that all her thoughts and memories of Everett scattered like puzzle pieces tossed across a coffee table. She couldn't remember why she had loved him. She couldn't remember what it was about him she found attractive. All she knew was that she found Chas *incredibly* attractive.

And some days, really strange days, the air between them seemed to be filled with energy and life enough that it was a living, breathing entity of its own. Still, seducing him or allowing herself to be seduced would be insane. Particularly since it was apparent he had two diametrically opposed opinions of her. He liked her looks, but he didn't like her personally.

As if to confirm the fact, Chas said, "Placing an ad is beyond the scope of Lily's duties...."

"Since she offered, she should be allowed to do it," Grant said simply, striding to the door. "Take care of the kids," he said, then left Chas and Lily standing alone in the echoing foyer.

Neither of them moved or spoke for at least a minute.

Finally Lily cleared her throat. "Is there anything you'd like me to do right now?"

Chas let out a long sigh. "Lily, you work day and night as it is. Can't you take a break? Did you have to volunteer to be Grant's secretary, too?"

"I didn't volunteer to be his secretary," Lily replied, confused. "I said I'd place an ad in the paper."

Chas sighed again. "I know. I'm sorry. Look, I'm going to go watch some TV." He turned and began to make his escape to the family room, but because she stood silently in the foyer, he stopped and faced her. "Would you like to watch some, too?" he asked reluctantly.

Lily licked her dry lips. There wasn't anything to do on this mountain. They didn't even have cable, so TV wasn't all that much of a treat. But right now it was better than nothing.

"I could watch some TV."

"Good. Great," he said, but if his tone was anything to go by, Lily sincerely doubted that he meant it.

She waited until they were settled and both were half-heartedly interested in a sitcom before she said, "You know, I thought that we'd come to some kind of a truce."

Staring at the television set, Chas said, "We did."

"Well, if we did, you're violating it." She knew it was foolish and idealistic, but she suddenly got the fanciful notion that if she could just get him to talk to her a little bit and get to know her, maybe he could also get to like her. "Because now you're the one who won't look at me or talk to me."

He blinked a few times, then peered at her. "Lily, this is a very difficult situation for me."

"I can understand that it's odd to have a new person in your house," Lily said. "But I'm here to make your life easier."

"You do anything but make my life easier," Chas said, then drew in a long fortifying breath. "You make my life amazingly complex," he said, looking directly at her as if to prove the sincerity of his words. "I'm trying to become a respected lawyer in a conservative town. It isn't good for my reputation to have you here, because everybody knows I have a weakness for pretty women."

Lily stared at him. "So the problem isn't me?"

"Hell, yes, it's you," Chas said, sounding angry again. "Look at you. You're gorgeous. But more than that, you're wonderful with the kids. You're thoughtful with me and Grant. Inside, Lily Andersen, you have a heart of gold."

He said it as if it were an accusation, and Lily laughed. "Well, thank you, I think."

"You're welcome," he muttered, trying to force himself to be interested in the television show again.

But though Lily didn't push him into further discussion, her thoughts didn't go anywhere near the sitcom. Chas might think he liked her only because she was pretty, but his feelings for her went beyond physical attraction. In the same way that she instantly, instinctively knew many things about him, partly from the way he treated the triplets, partly from his respect for Grant, partly from the pro bono legal work he did, he could discern the good things in her, too.

And that's what bothered him. He was as drawn to her as she was to him. He might try to mask his real feelings by calling them sexual attraction or lust, but he'd inadvertently admitted the truth to her...even if he couldn't admit it to himself.

He *liked* her.

Fear unexpectedly poured through her. Even without knowing that Chas had been divorced twice, any clear-thinking woman would see he wasn't a man to play with. Intense, serious, abundantly endowed with sex appeal, Chas could seduce her with only half of his charm. If he used full power, she'd probably melt.

Since he couldn't admit to himself that he liked her, and she had feelings that carried her away like a runaway train, then this man could hurt her. And unless she got a hold of herself, for good, for real, forever, she was in for another heartbreak.

Chapter Five

"Hello, Mrs. Pawlowski," Lily said as she opened the front door. "Mr. Brewster's expecting you," she added, taking Ginny's coat and hat and hanging them in a closet on the way to the den. She led Mrs. Pawlowski into the study, and announced her to Chas, who sat behind the big mahogany desk looking very sophisticated in his tweed coat, white oxford cloth shirt and black trousers.

As Chas offered Mrs. Pawlowski a seat, Lily smiled at him, then left the den, closing the door behind her.

In the hall, she heaved a huge sigh. Though two weeks had passed since she realized she and Chas found each other attractive on more than a physical level, and she felt much more in control, she hadn't been able to do anything about her feelings for him. She knew beyond a shadow of a doubt that if she let her emotions get away from her, he'd hurt her, but she also didn't know how to put the brakes on them. There were hundreds of reasons to like Chas, not counting his looks and sex appeal.

Most centered on the fact that he was a genuinely nice guy trying to make his way in the shadow of two highly successful brothers, and trying to deal with the grief of losing his parents while he raised three kids.

It was perfectly understandable that she would have a soft spot for him, that she would do everything she could to help him, and that forming that kind of bond would make her like him more. But, even though she couldn't seem to do anything about her feelings, at least she no longer felt she was losing her marbles.

Chas, however, felt as if he had completely lost his. One smile, one slightly above-average smile from Lily and his train of thought had gone out the window. It took him five minutes of small talk with Mrs. Pawlowski before he could gather his wits enough to address the legal problems she faced becoming the guardian of her granddaughter.

And the minute Mrs. Pawlowski walked out the front door, Lily robbed him of rational thought again just by pleasantly asking him to help her feed the babies.

Today she wore tight jeans, a sweatshirt and white tennis shoes without socks, and with her blond hair pulled into a loose ponytail, she looked youthful and happy. After a little over three weeks of living at Brewster Mansion, her reserve was gone and in its place was a contentedness and confidence that made her an absolute joy to have around and left Chas with a warm, contented feeling of his own. A feeling that started in the pit of his stomach and seemed to spiral outward—a feeling that felt so damned much like happiness it scared him. He remembered this feeling all too well; the very same feeling had led him down the aisle to matrimony twice. The very same feeling had landed him in jail once.

Was it any wonder he didn't trust it?

"You feed Taylor, I'll feed Annie," Lily instructed, directing him to take the seat in front of Taylor's high chair. "Between bites, both of us will manage Cody."

Because it was a system Chas and his brothers had invented, he didn't argue. He simply sat, picked up Taylor's kitty spoon and eyed the luncheon plate of mashed green stuff, lumpy off-white stuff, and dull-looking purple stuff.

"Yum," he said to Taylor, though he recognized there was a definite lack of enthusiasm in his voice.

"It is yum to them," Lily scolded cheerfully, but when she glanced at him she frowned. "You'd better change. If you get plums or peas on that white shirt, I may not be able to get them out."

Chas peered down at his shirt. "I'm fine."

Though he thought she might argue, Lily only shrugged. "Suit yourself. But you can't say I didn't warn you."

"I consider myself warned," Chas said, sliding Taylor's spoon along the edge of the off-white lumpy stuff. "What is this?" he asked carefully, trying to keep the skepticism out of his voice.

"It's macaroni."

"From a jar?"

"Well, you can buy it in a jar, and I'm sure the kids have eaten it from a jar, but I made this myself in the food processor. I mashed the peas, too."

Chas looked at it with a fresh eye. "So it's real food?"

Annie responded to Chas's comment with a loud screech as if she didn't appreciate him criticizing her dinner.

"All their food is real food," Lily protested with a giggle.

"I know it's real food. And I'm sure it's delicious," he added, speaking directly to Annie, who gave him a semitoothless grin. "But frankly, it all looks the same to me."

"True, but it tastes different," Lily said. "Right, Cody?"

Cody yelped and pounded the palm of his hand on his high chair tray.

"See, Cody loves it," Lily said, then fed him a bite of macaroni. He smacked his lips delightedly.

"I take it we're saving the purple stuff for last," Chas said, this time dipping Taylor's kitty spoon in the smooth green concoction.

"It's plums for dessert," Lily confirmed, her attention absorbed in feeding Annie. "That I didn't make. I got it from a jar, but it's one of their favorites."

"I always liked the bananas," Chas said. "Years ago," he began, then he laughed. "Decades ago, actually, my mother's sister would spend two weeks with us every summer. Because we lived so far out in the country, her kids, my cousins, thought of this house and the surrounding grounds as something like a resort."

Listening as she fed Annie, Lily smiled. "I come from the city. I can see how they'd draw that conclusion."

"Anyway, it seemed like every year my aunt had a new baby. And every year my mother would go out and stock up on baby food. When I was about four I remember Grant stealing a few jars. Since the babies liked it so much, he figured there was something special about it. We gagged on most of the varieties, but the mashed bananas were very good."

Though Chas had continued to feed Taylor while telling his story, Taylor grew impatient with the fact that his attention wasn't completely focused on her, and she yelped loudly and pounded her fist on the tray of her high chair. Unfortunately, the heel of her hand caught the edge of her dish and sent it flying in the air. Chas watched in complete horror as the dish did three midair rotations then landed on his shirt front.

"Take that off this minute," Lily said, bounding from her seat. She ran to the sink and grabbed a damp cloth. "If those peas or those plums set, that shirt is ruined."

"I'm not so much worried about the shirt as I am the jacket," Chas said, stripping off the coat with ease.

Lily immediately scrubbed at the few specks that had landed on his lapel. When it was cleaned, she glanced at his shirt and groaned. "Oh, Taylor, look what you did!"

"Did," Taylor repeated, giggling.

Chas laughed, too. "I'll 'did' you one," he said, but he chuckled. "They're just like parrots," he said, as he began to unbutton the cuffs of his shirt. "They can repeat bits and pieces of words, but they don't have a clue about what they're saying."

"You think this is funny," Lily said. "Wait until they start repeating your swear words."

"I don't swear," Chas objected, making short order of the buttons of his shirt. "Grant swears."

"My sister had a neighbor who once called her on the carpet because she claimed Mary Louise's boys had sworn around her angel children, and she simply couldn't abide that," Lily said, giving Chas's jacket another quick once-over as she waited for him to remove his shirt. "But the next day, the neighbor's four-year-old called Mary Louise to the fence and let out a line so crude my sister almost fainted. Then in a whisper the little girl told Mary Louise that her mother said that all the time. That's the poetic justice of children. You can't be a hypocrite.''

Laughing, Chas unbuttoned the last button of his shirt and stripped it off without thinking. He crumpled it in a ball and tossed it over Lily's head onto the washer in the laundry room, but the second the shirt became airborne, he realized what he'd done. He was standing shirtless in the kitchen with a woman he was so attracted to he could spit, and there wasn't an ounce of protection anywhere.

Chas looked at Lily. Lily looked at Chas. He'd never felt so naked in his entire life. Though he'd paraded completely nude in front of two wives, suddenly, without a shirt, still wearing pants, he felt completely exposed.

He cleared his throat. "Let's just get my shirt into the washer."

"I'll do it," Lily said, rushing forward at the same time he took a step toward the laundry room. They would have bumped into each other, except Lily stopped her forward progress by placing her palms flat against his chest.

Chas sucked air between his teeth and jumped back as if she'd burned him, but Lily stood staring at his chest as if she'd never seen a naked man before. Puzzled, Chas forgot all about his wayward reactions and watched her as she seemed to marvel at the hair on his chest. She looked at his chest, his shoulders, his biceps, his forearms…all the way down to his hands. Then her gaze drifted until she was staring at his abdomen. Chas stifled the urge to suck in his stomach and puff out his chest, and he was glad that he had because it was apparent that without any enhancements or augmentation, she liked what she saw.

Unfortunately, once he realized that, his body started reacting again. He cleared his throat. "You take care of the laundry and I'll go grab a fresh shirt."

"Okay," she said, but she didn't move, only continued to stare at him.

Chas gritted his teeth. Damn it! She was all but begging him to kiss her. That wonderful, mesmerized expression called to every male instinct he had. It stroked his ego, inflated his pride. It made him feel big and strong and...well, virile.

Virile! Good Lord, that one was trouble. Suddenly he pivoted and headed for the kitchen door.

He would control this. He had sworn to himself that he would control this, and by Heaven he would.

Lily didn't even try to hide the fact that seeing Chas without a shirt had thrown her for a loop. Now she understood why being around him made thoughts of Everett scatter like leaves from a tree. Chas was perfect. Not that Everett was horribly flawed, but he was a far cry from perfect. He had been her first date, her first kiss, her first love, her first lover. In a certain sense, she was only now realizing there were other fish in the sea. And the first fish she met just happened to have a beautiful body, gray-green eyes that could see the whole way into a woman's soul and a laugh that filled her with joy. He was everything any woman would want. It was no wonder she was smitten.

And having the devil's time hiding it.

"Are we going to bathe the children together?" Chas asked as he scooped up a squirming baby with one arm and hoisted another to his shoulder, balancing her against the palm of his large hand. Because Evan and Claire had returned, one or both of them came to the house to pick up Cody every night after work, leaving Chas and Lily with only two baby girls until morning.

"Yes," Lily said, but she swallowed. She'd never thought much about the size of a man's hands before, but seeing Chas's hands, the easy way he could manage an eighteen-pound child with his wide palms and long, lean fingers, Lily got a jolt of something she understood perfectly. She could almost feel those big hands smoothing up her naked back, or spanning her waist, or massaging her shoulders.

"Okay, what time are we going to do this?"

Lily quickly pulled herself together. "How about eight?"

Carrying his two giggling kids into the family room, Chas said, "That gives me a whole hour to proof this brief if you don't mind entertaining them alone."

"No! No!" Lily said, and though she knew she sounded overanxious and probably crazy, she didn't care. A few minutes alone with the babies was exactly what she needed.

Entering the family room behind him, she waited as he tossed the girls into the play yard.

"You're sure this is all right?" he asked, turning and catching her as she gazed at his profile.

She felt her cheeks catch fire. "Yes. I'm fine," she said, trying to sound professional.

Chas nodded briefly. "Good. Then I'll see you in about an hour."

Smiling as calmly as she could, Lily nodded.

When he was gone, she sank into a chair. With the girls sufficiently occupied with stuffed bears, chew toys and each other, she closed her eyes and pulled her lower lip between her teeth. The damnedest part of this was, she didn't want to stop her reactions. Oh, she knew she should. But she wasn't quite ready yet. No one had ever had this powerful effect on her. She had the oddest sensation that feelings like this came along once in a lifetime. If she ignored them or avoided them, she would lose them.

But even though she was beginning to suspect her feelings for Everett had been sadly lacking, she couldn't jeopardize her job.

She had to get herself in line.

When Chas returned to the family room an hour later and made her laugh with the way he stacked the girls on his arms and treated them to a ''ride'' up the steps, Lily forgot she was supposed to be monitoring her reactions. As they bathed the children, he told her outlandish tales of the horrible embarrassment of having to call his brothers to bail him out of jail, and she laughed with him because he was beginning to be able to laugh at himself. When they took the kids to the rockers to feed them a last bottle before bedtime and he moved on to whispering stories of being cold, hungry and alone in law school, her entire heart sympathized. And when he tucked the last baby in her crib, kissed her forehead and wished her pleasant dreams, her heart melted.

Chas wasn't entirely sure what to make of this situation, but he did know he was no longer getting mixed signals. Lily was as interested in him as he was in her.

The way he had this figured, over a month had gone by since she'd lost her fiancé and in man world that meant she should be getting on with the rest of her life. It was time. Though she had skipped the drinking binge, one rowdy night in town and at least two fist fights, Chas decided women probably had their own grieving rituals, and she'd probably already completed hers.

Outside the nursery door he took two steps toward his bedroom, but stopped and faced her again. "You wouldn't feel like cards or TV or something tonight, would you?"

She gave him her smitten kitten look again, the one that seemed to reach the whole way into his solar plexus and redefine his opinion of himself, a welcome addition to his life.

"I'm really not much good with cards."

"Television?" he asked hopefully.

She shrugged. "I'm not much on TV, either. Why don't we just make some cocoa and talk."

He stared at her. "Talk?"

"You know. Share ideas, concepts, tell stories. I'm sure you've heard of it. You were doing it the whole time we bathed the kids. Some people call it conversation."

"I know what conversation is. It's just that I usually talk while I'm doing something else."

"Really?" she said, looking at him as if he'd just proposed a new religion.

He ran his hand along the back of his neck. "Look, forget I said anything."

"No. No," she said, grabbing his hand and tugging on it to get him to move toward the stairs. "You're right. We can't just run off to our separate rooms for the rest of my stay here. We're the only entertainment we've got. I'll try this card thing of yours, but you're going to have to teach me, so pick a simple game."

He chose rummy. Not gin, but five hundred. The first four hands they made matches of only three of a kind until she got the hang of the game. When he was sure she had that down, he told her about three-card straights.

She stared at him as if dumbfounded. "Three different cards, like a six, seven, eight could be a match?"

"Yes," he agreed cautiously. "But only if they belong to the same suit. You remember the clubs, hearts, diamonds and spades?"

She nodded.

"Well, you get a six, seven and eight of spades, and you've got a match. Or six, seven and eight of diamonds and that's a match."

"Or two, three and four of clubs."

He beamed. "Exactly."

"Okay," she said, motioning with her hands that he could deal the cards again. "I'm ready."

"Now," Chas said, passing out the cards. "What are you going to be looking for?"

"Cards from the same suit and cards of the same type, like all threes."

"Good," he said, "you're ready."

She picked up her cards and from the look on her face, Chas could see she was concentrating in earnest. Because he had dealt, it was her turn first and she took a card from the top of the stack, slid it into her hand, shifted a card or two around, then gasped with delight.

"I'm out!" she cried and set her hand on the table.

Chas peered at it, and sighed with frustration. "You're not out. Not all your cards are used."

"Sure they are," she happily disagreed. "The six, seven and eight of diamonds are a match. Then I have three eights. Then I have an eight, nine and ten of clubs."

"Yes," Chas agreed, trying to be patient. "But you can't use the cards from one match in another match."

"I didn't."

"Sure you did. Two of those eights belong to three-card straight matches." He pulled the two eights away, clustering them into their straights and showed her that she had a card left that didn't make a match.

She frowned.

"Here," he magnanimously offered. "We'll just forget that and start all over."

"But I had two matches," she said indignantly.

"But you also had an eight that stood alone."

"Technically, it wasn't alone. It matched the other two eights."

"True. But because you'd already used the other eights in other matches, you couldn't use them again," Chas patiently explained one more time.

"All right," Lily said, sounding frustrated now. "Let's just try again."

Chas dealt the cards. The hand continued for three rounds of play, then Lily set her cards down, again claiming victory.

Unfortunately, she was wrong again, and Chas explained why, somewhat angrily.

"I don't think I want to play if you're going to yell at me."

He drew a quick breath. "I'm not yelling."

"Well, you're not yelling-yelling, but you just seem like you're getting angry or something."

"I'm not getting angry," he said through gritted teeth.

"I think we are," Lily said, singsonging her words as if she were talking with one of the triplets, but rather than sit and wait for his rebuttal, she rose and began gathering the cards. When she walked to his side of the game table, he caught her wrist before she could step away.

"I don't appreciate being treated like one of the kids."

"Then don't act like one," she said smartly.

"Oh, I get it. That means you want me to do what you've been begging me to do all day long."

That caused her to peer at him. "What's that?"

"Don't give me that innocent act."

"I don't have a clue what you're talking about," she said imperially.

"Then I'll be happy to show you."

Before she knew what he was about, Chas rose, pulled her against him and pressed his mouth to hers.

Chapter Six

Lily had feelings that started at her middle and spiraled outward the whole way to her toes. With Chas's hands grasping her upper arms, pulling her hard against him and his mouth plundering hers, Lily experienced things she thought only happened in the movies. She was drawn to his masculinity. She was awed by the controlled strength that coiled through him. And she wanted to match him. This wasn't like the competition over the housework. No, this was a force of nature that coursed through her, an instinct as old as time itself. She didn't seem to be able to stop it or temper it, but then again, she didn't really want to. She reveled in this feeling that was part desire, part pure femininity.

He made her feel more like a woman in thirty seconds than Everett had made her feel in six years.

The thought of Everett stopped her cold. Though she sincerely doubted that rebounding could be this intense or this wonderful, she also wasn't stupid. She knew she shouldn't get involved with anyone too quickly after such a devastating breakup.

She pulled away. He immediately apologized, running his hand along the back of his neck. "Look, I'm sorry. That won't ever happen again."

"You're sorry?" she asked, confused.

"Well, it's obvious you didn't want me to kiss you."

Lily couldn't help herself, she smiled. "That's not exactly the way I remember it."

He peered at her. "Then what happened?"

"Chas, I just came out of a six-year relationship. I genuinely thought Everett was the love of my life. Now, even though I know he wasn't, I can't just jump into something without a little thought."

"And you shouldn't," Chas agreed, occupying himself with gathering the cards. He'd never felt like such an idiot. He had let his emotions get away from him, and unless he took hold of the situation, he might do permanent damage to their working relationship—a relationship he needed much more than a romantic one. Though he had to admit, she was one hell of a kisser and she had him aching in places he didn't know could ache. Still, all things considered, that kiss had been a mistake and now he had to fix it.

"Not only should you give yourself a little time to heal," he counseled, as if he hadn't been the culprit who kissed her, "but you also should consider that you and Everett aren't through. Nobody gives up six years without a word," he added, sliding the cards into their container.

"He gave me plenty of words," Lily said softly. "He gave me a six-page letter."

"But you never had a face-to-face confrontation, right?"

She shook her head.

"I rest my case," Chas said victoriously. "Until you have that face-to-face conversation, there is no closure." He snapped the lid on the cards, stored them in a drawer, and turned to her again. "We can continue the rummy game tomorrow, if you'd like," he suggested formally. "If you decide you're not interested in learning, I'll understand that, too. Right now, I think I'm going to see if I can't get a few hours of sleep before one of the babies needs me. Good night."

"Good night," Lily said, watching him go. Once his footsteps had faded away, her face scrunched in confusion. She knew he'd wanted to kiss her. She'd felt unleashed passion resonating through him—at least she thought she had. After one kiss from Chas she was beginning to see that her vast sexual experience wasn't vast at all, and, in fact, would probably be considered limited. The truth of the matter was she could have imagined his response to her. Given that he'd run out of the room so quickly, the logical conclusion would be that she'd misinterpreted him. That he hadn't wanted to kiss her. Or maybe he'd kissed her as a test and the feelings he'd anticipated weren't there. And maybe she'd failed the test.

The hurt of rejection washed over her, and Lily swallowed hard, but she straightened her shoulders and marched to her room. If getting left at the altar hadn't defeated her, being rejected after one kiss wasn't going to accomplish the task, either.

She'd lived through absolutely the most humiliating thing that could happen to her. Chas deciding she wasn't worth pursuing was nothing. Nothing at all to get upset about. It might hurt like the dickens and make her eyes sting with unexpected tears, but she refused to get upset.

Unfortunately, the minute she was behind the closed door of her room, the tears she'd been holding at bay fell in earnest. She cried because she was embarrassed. She cried because she felt witless and stupid and young.

Then she cried because she *didn't* miss Everett. Not at all. Not even a little bit. If she had, she wouldn't have fallen like a rock for Chas.

Having such a severe reaction to one brief kiss reminded Lily that she was supposed to be thinking about more than the present. True, it was important to do a good job and it was important that she got along with her employers, but she was also supposed to be setting new goals, deciding her path, figuring out a plan for the rest of her life.

And if she interpreted what he'd said correctly, Chas had also wanted the security of a plan after his mother had died, when he and his brothers had struck out on their own. Just like her, when the chips were down, he tried to strategize his way out of his problems.

It was easy to see that they were very much alike and because of that, Lily forgave herself for falling for him. They had enough in common that they had become fast friends. Being attracted to each other made them want to expand on those feelings. So he'd kissed her. Big deal.

Actually, Lily had to admit on her way to the diner the following Sunday afternoon, it was a big deal. In spite of the fact that she knew it was wrong, her feelings for Chas grew stronger and stronger every day. When she looked at him, she saw a good father for her children. She saw somebody she could talk with honestly and openly. Now she was beginning to see the house with the picket fence. She genuinely believed all this wasn't because she was rebounding. But it had happened too fast to trust. Even if Chas hadn't changed his mind about his feelings for her, she would have had to stop, control or ignore these feelings somehow.

Luckily, he'd changed his mind.

"What can I get for you?"

Lily looked up from the menu she was reading to see Abby, the waitress who also ran the bed and breakfast she'd stayed at. The woman was tall, with voluminous red hair tied back in a bright pink ribbon. Her cherubic face was wreathed in a smile.

"I'm really not hungry. I just needed somewhere to go to get out of the house."

Abby grinned broadly. "Not many places to go here in Brewster County," she agreed, swiping a cloth over the surface of the counter. "But on Sunday afternoons a lot of people like to come in for a piece of pie. That's pretty much the norm here in Brewster. Where did you say you were from?"

"Wisconsin," Lily replied. "I left because I needed a change of pace and ran out of money here," she admitted wryly.

Abby burst out laughing and poured Lily a cup of coffee. "At least you have an excuse. Some of us were born here and stayed anyway."

"Oh, it's not that bad," Lily said hurriedly, afraid she'd offended Abby.

"Honey, I know that. I stay here because I like it. It's quiet and peaceful. It's how I want to live."

"Me, too," Lily agreed, then got a little more comfortable on her stool. "I never told you this when I left the bed and breakfast, but I took the job as the nanny for the Brewster triplets."

Abby eyed her with unabashed curiosity. "Claire said

they'd hired someone. She even mentioned the woman was very pretty. I should have guessed it was you. Since you're new in town and probably celebrating your new job,'' she added cheerfully. ''A slice of apple pie is on the house.''

''Thank you,'' Lily said, taking a sip of coffee when Abby walked away to get her pie.

''Mind if I sit here?''

Lily turned to see a man in his sixties sliding onto the stool beside her.

''Sure, no problem,'' she said sweetly.

''I'm Arnie Garrett,'' he said, introducing himself and offering her his hand to shake. ''The local attorney.''

''Oh, then you probably know Chas Brewster, one of the men I work for. He's a lawyer, too.''

''Hell, I know all the Brewster boys. I was their father's best friend…God rest his soul. Not only did I watch those boys grow up, but I'm very well acquainted with the triplets, too. How are they doing, anyway?''

''They're fine. Wonderful,'' Lily said. ''I was unbelievably lucky to get this job.''

Arnie Garrett smiled. ''They were unbelievably lucky to get you,'' he said. ''I can't imagine two bachelors caring for three kids.''

''They don't care for three kids,'' Lily said, then sipped her coffee. ''Evan and Claire take Cody every night. Chas and Grant only care for the girls.''

''Really?'' Arnie said, sounding confused. ''Still, those girls must be a handful for two men.''

''No, they're great with the kids,'' Lily said. ''I've never seen men try so hard.''

Without warning Arnie rose, tossed a few dollars on the counter and said, ''Well, it was very nice to meet you. I'm sure I'll see you again.''

"Goodbye," Lily said, waving as he left the diner. When she turned back to the counter, Abby set a piece of pie in front of her.

"I warmed it in the microwave for you," she said proudly. "And added a scoop of ice cream."

"Thank you," Lily said, sniffing the sweet, cinnamon aroma.

"Actually, the pie's not free," Abby said, but she laughed. "It will cost you some information. You have to tell me everything about yourself so I can head off the town busybodies."

"If I tell you everything about myself you won't be able to ward off the busybodies," Lily said, then she sighed. She wasn't 100 percent sure why, but she trusted Abby. Not only did she have a kind face, but her warm, genuine personality made Lily feel more relaxed than she had in months. "A few weeks before I came here, my fiancé left me at the altar."

Abby only stared at her. "No kidding."

"I wish I were."

"Ouch."

"More ouch than you will ever know."

"Feel like talking about it?" Abby asked sympathetically.

"I don't think I'm quite there yet," Lily admitted. "But I'll be back for pie again," she said, took a bite and groaned with pleasure. "By then you probably won't be able to shut me up."

In her car on the drive home, Lily calculated that she had over a thousand dollars saved. Not only were the Brewsters generous with salary, but they provided room and board. She didn't have a clue how much it would cost to go to school, didn't know if she'd be able to support herself while she attended classes or if she'd need money for that, too, but there was plenty of time to worry about those details.

Just like there was plenty of time to try to sort out why she felt such strong emotions for Chas. She didn't agree that she would see Everett again. The very thought made her shudder because her first instinct was to want to sock him for embarrassing her, which was proof positive that there were no residual feelings to worry about.

But she did understand what Chas had said about giving herself time, and she agreed with him. She may not need as much healing time as everyone thought, but she definitely wanted to think long and hard before she started a relationship. If she was going to protect herself from another mistake, she needed to figure out why she'd fallen so hard and so fast for Chas. But more than that—particularly now that she knew he didn't share her feelings—she had to make him believe she wasn't attracted to him. Which meant she had to keep her wayward hormones under control.

Not an easy feat now that she knew how fabulous his kisses were and how much like a woman she felt in the arms of the right man.

"I hope you don't mind, but I invited Claire and Evan to dinner tonight," Chas said to Lily as she entered the kitchen. Coming into the warm house after spending time in the cool October air had brightened her cheeks. In spite of the fact that she was bundled in a bulky baby-blue sweater and thick navy-blue leggings, she shivered inside them. "We like having the triplets together as much as possible, and since I was cooking, I didn't think it would be a problem."

"I don't mind at all. I love the company," she said, emphasizing the last sentence, and Chas hoped she didn't love company because she felt she needed protection from him, just as he hoped she hadn't needed an afternoon out of the house because she didn't want to be around him anymore.

"So, where did you go all afternoon?" he asked, busying himself by stirring his spaghetti sauce.

Lily shrugged again. "Nowhere really."

"You just rode around?" he asked, trying not to pry, but holding his curiosity at bay only with shear force of will. "Didn't stop anywhere? Didn't see anyone?"

"Actually, I saw two people. I went to the diner, and Abby gave me free pie, then an older gentleman sat down beside me and introduced himself."

Some guy who probably got a cheap thrill simply from being close to someone as gorgeous as Lily, Chas thought.

"It was weird, though," Lily continued, sneaking a bite of lettuce from the salad Chas had prepared. "He seemed almost eager to talk, then suddenly jumped up and left."

At that Chas frowned. "Are you sure you didn't imagine that?"

She shook her head. "No. In fact, now that I think about it, it was almost as if he wanted to get away before Abby returned."

Chas peered at her. "You have an awfully suspicious mind."

"Try getting left at the altar sometime," Lily suggested blithely. "It leaves you with all kinds of strange thoughts and conclusions."

"No doubt," Chas agreed. Not wanting to pursue that line of conversation any further, he brought the original topic back. "You said the guy introduced himself. What was his name?"

"Averie...Artie...Arnie! That's it. Arnie Gavett or something like that. Said he was a lawyer."

"Arnie Garrett." Chas stopped stirring and faced her. "I'll bet he asked about the triplets, didn't he?"

"Yes. Yes, he did."

"Terrific."

Lily gave him a curious look. "What's wrong? Did I do something wrong?"

"No, my brothers and I did something wrong by not warning you about Arnie Garrett."

"Is he the local pervert or something?"

"No," Chas said with a sigh. "He's the trustee of the triplet's inheritance if my brothers and I don't want to raise them."

"Or if you *can't* raise them," Lily said with a groan. "He was pumping me for information, wasn't he? Oh, I'm sorry."

"It's not your fault," Chas said, but he blew his breath out on another long sigh. "It's just that it's been over four months and we really hadn't heard anything from him. He hasn't filed any papers or attempted to take the triplets away from us in any way at all, and I guess we forgot about him."

"You think he's interested again?"

"I think he'll be interested until the kids turn twenty-one. Until then, if he can become their legal guardian, he not only gets control of half of the lumber mill, but he also would draw a salary from the kids' money."

"That jerk."

"Actually, it's a perfectly legal, perfectly necessary arrangement for kids who don't have a guardian. But our kids have a guardian. They have *three* guardians."

"I'll bet Mr. Garrett wouldn't mind getting the money, though," Lily speculated, and Chas thought about her comment for the rest of the time it took him to prepare dinner. When Claire and Evan arrived with Cody, Grant and Lily escorted them into the family room with the girls and Chas forgot to worry about Grant and Lily being together. His mind was too focused on Arnie Garrett. So much so that after everyone was seated and dinner was well underway, he said, "Lily met Arnie Garrett in town this afternoon."

Grant set his fork down. "You did?"

"Yes. Abby offered me a piece of pie, and while she was in the kitchen getting it, Mr. Garrett sat beside me."

"And asked about the triplets," Evan guessed quietly.

"Yes. But as quickly as he sat down, he left again."

"Because Abby was returning," Chas added, sending both of his brothers a clear message with his facial expression.

Grant drew a long breath. "You think he's up to something?"

"Maybe," Chas said.

"Great," Grant said, tossing his napkin onto the table. "This is the last thing we need right now. We can't spare Evan from the mill. You need time to establish yourself," he said to Chas. "And I'm divided between here and Savannah. There isn't anybody left to fight him."

"Well, I was thinking about that," Chas said, spinning his fork through his spaghetti without actually gathering any. "We wouldn't have to fight him if we could strike up some sort of deal with him, offer him a settlement."

Grant only stared at him. "Never."

Evan shook his head in concurrence. "I don't think so, either."

"Good," Chas said, sighing with relief. "I only mentioned it because it is an option."

"No, it's not," Grant said, and turned his attention back to his food. "As long as we are available for these kids and we're taking good care of them, Arnie doesn't have a leg to stand on. And there are five of us now," he added, glancing around the table. "Five of us to care for three kids. There's no way in hell he can say we're neglecting them."

Although Lily didn't argue that, she had a sinking feeling in the pit of her stomach. Going over that two-minute episode in the diner, she remembered the unholy gleam that came to Arnie's eyes when she mentioned that Claire and Evan cared for Cody. She didn't know enough about the law to ascertain if that was trouble. She only knew that she was the one who had spilled the beans, and she felt horrible. Chas, Grant and Evan didn't want to care for these kids because they owned half the lumber mill or because they were entitled to half the profits from the mill, but because they loved them. And if they lost the triplets because of something she said today, she would never forgive herself.

Chas found her pacing in the family room after ten o'clock. From the tortured, torn expression on her lovely face, he knew exactly what she was thinking about.

"Lily, really," he said softly, capturing her attention and prompting her to face him. "What happened with you and Arnie Garrett today wasn't your fault. If anyone should have thought to warn you about him, it's me."

"I know, but I still shouldn't have said anything."

"You shouldn't have said you work for us?" Chas asked wryly, stifling a grin.

She shook her head. "No. I'm talking about blabbering on about what good caregivers you were, and how Evan and Claire care for Cody individually. If he's going to find anything to use in what I said, it's that."

"What? That we give Cody special attention? How is he going to find fault with that?"

"Maybe by suggesting to a court that triplets need to be kept together?"

"The triplets are together. I'd argue that in any court. We only separate them so each one of them gets a few hours of special, individualized attention...which I believe they need. I'd argue that, too."

"You would?" Lily asked hopefully.

"Hell, yeah," Chas said, sitting on the arm of the sofa, watching her as she continued to pace. "I don't know if there's case law in Pennsylvania about it, but it probably all boils down to an argument about the definition of the word *together*. In our situation the kids usually eat breakfast and lunch together. They spend the morning playing together, then nap together. After lunch they play together again and nap again. If a court doesn't think that's together enough, the worst-case scenario would be that Evan and Claire would move back into the mansion. Then everybody's together twenty-four hours a day again."

Lily visibly relaxed. "It's that simple?"

"Lily, *everything's* that simple on paper. The difficult part would be getting the five adults involved in the babies' care to share three bathrooms. But even that could be solved," he suggested merrily. "We'd just do a little remodeling."

At that she laughed. "You're not making fun of me are you?"

"Nope. I'm telling you exactly how I'd handle the problem if Arnie were to use the argument that the kids weren't living together."

She stopped pacing and gazed at him. "And you have it all figured out?"

"Of course. A good lawyer always knows both sides of the case," he said, then he laughed. "Boy, you are one softhearted cookie, aren't you?"

"I think it's my downfall. You know how people always say your best trait is also your Achilles' heel? Well, caring too much is mine."

Chas considered that. "I don't think I've ever met anybody who cared too much before."

Lily raised her hand as if answering a question in school. "Well, you have now. Here I am."

"No. I think you're missing what I'm saying. As the valedictorian of the Stupid in Love Club, I cannot imagine that it's possible to have someone care too much about me. I can see how someone interfering and offering unsolicited advice would be a problem. But I can't see how good, old-fashioned caring could be a problem." He paused, considered again, then said, "In fact, I think I rather like it."

"Yeah, tell me that again when I'm reminding you to put your boots on after the first light snowfall."

Chas smiled at the image that that summoned forth. "I'd probably kiss your nose. Or nip your nose. I'd be like Jack Frost nipping at your nose. Then I'd probably go out without my boots."

"And I'd nurse your cold."

He rather liked the thought of that, too, but he said, "The theory that people get colds from wet feet is an old wives' tale."

She only sniffed a response to that, and he laughed. "Don't ever change. I mean that," he said, and rose from his seat and walked over to her. "That Everett guy might not have appreciated you, but you are truly a treasure." He put his palms on her cheeks and lifted her face until she was looking at him. "And I'm very, very glad Grant forced me to hire you," he said, before he lowered his head and kissed her.

Where the first kiss had been filled with passion and suppressed longing, this kiss was soft, gentle and as abundant with emotion as a spring rain. He no longer believed he instinctively, intuitively knew things about this woman. "Knowing" had nothing to do with any part of what he felt. He had gone beyond knowing and had somehow tumbled into a realm or place where knowing was a shallow, inadequate way to interact. He had jumped from knowing to appreciating. In a matter of a few short weeks, he felt as if he'd found a friend. A true friend. Someone he could trust with his life. Someone he could trust even more than his brothers…or maybe differently from the way he trusted his brothers.

A warm sensation rippled through him. He'd never met anyone who was so damned nice to have around. He'd never *liked* anyone as much as he liked her.

Lily pulled away, gazed at him with her large, round, blue eyes and drew a long breath. "I thought we'd decided it wasn't wise for us to be kissing."

He thought about that. Not from his vantage point, but from hers. Lily had much more to lose than he did if they attempted a relationship and it didn't work out. But he knew in his heart that it would work out. Because this pairing had the ingredient missing from all his other matches. Friendship.

"I'm not going to hurt you."

"You're right about that," she agreed. "Because I'm not going to let you. My heart's just been broken, Chas. My life's in complete disarray. The last thing I need right now is to get involved with someone." She looked him right in the eye. "Or worse, to *not* get involved with someone."

She turned and walked out of the room without saying good-night, and Chas cursed roundly under his breath. Unless he misinterpreted what she'd said, she didn't want a permanent relationship with him, but she also didn't want a casual fling.

She had just completely rejected him.

Chapter Seven

Chas wasn't the kind of person who minded rejection. Training to be a lawyer, he'd been taught that he would lose cases, he would lose clients and he would lose friends. And sometimes those losses would have nothing to do with justice. He could accept that. He knew the world wasn't supposed to be fair. But there was something about the way that Lily didn't even want to give this a try that bugged the hell out of him.

A few minutes before dawn he figured out what it was. His feelings for Jennifer had been lust, and his feelings for Gretchen had been insatiable lust. He'd loved Charlene, but he hadn't really known her. However, he felt he more than knew Lily. He appreciated her. He understood her. He *liked* her. He had gut instincts about her that hummed through his soul, reminded him of the good and decent parts of his nature, as well as the raw, passionate parts of his masculinity. She truly brought out the best in him.

He understood exactly what an accomplishment it was

to bring out his best, because he knew himself. He knew he wasn't a saint. He knew he wasn't perfect. He knew the sun didn't rise and set upon his world any more than anyone else's world, but he also knew that every man was entitled to choose a life and live it to the fullest, being the best he could be.

And that's what he wanted. A good life. Friends, family and a sense of purpose, all intertwined with a mutually beneficial relationship predicated upon friendship. And he genuinely believed that's what Lily wanted, too.

He acknowledged what she'd told him the night before. He wasn't discounting anything she said or even the validity of what she said, but he also recognized that she was afraid.

Not that he blamed her. If anybody understood her misgivings about a relationship, it was him. But that was what made him ideal for her.

All he had to do was make her see it wasn't merely possible for them to be together, it was *right* for them to be together.

She walked into the nursery when he had just finished dressing Taylor and was about to start on Annie. "I'll get her," she whispered. "You take Taylor downstairs."

This morning Lily wore her pink chenille robe over a pair of solid pink flannel pajamas. Her hair was sleep tousled and she was having difficulty opening her eyes, but to Chas she looked wonderful. Perfect. Like the woman he wanted to spend the rest of his life with.

Debating whether or not to kiss her, he smiled. "That's a good idea," he said, but didn't move.

Lily walked to Annie's crib and pulled her from the warmth of her covers. "Hello, little one. Let's get you into something nice and soft and feed you something yummy for breakfast."

Annie made soft gurgling noises, as if she wasn't exactly thrilled to be awake, but knew staying in bed wasn't the answer, either. Lily turned to carry her to the changing table and almost bumped into Chas.

"I thought you were going downstairs to wait for Cody."

He smiled stupidly. "I am."

She frowned at him. "Then go."

He let out a brief chuckle before he took Taylor out of the room. Lily stared at the door. Something was up. She could tell. Not that she wanted to be so perceptive about Chas. She was beginning to think that was another one of their downfalls. Because they had been through so many similar situations, they understood each other. They thought they knew each other. But last night before she'd fallen asleep, Lily had decided nothing could be further from the truth. They had met only a little over four weeks ago. There was no way they could know each other. And certainly no way they could "love" each other. But since they kept stumbling into accidentally intimate situations, they were reading everything all wrong.

Falling, when they weren't supposed to.

Which meant she had to be both alert and smart, and that's exactly what she intended to be. In case she'd misinterpreted Chas's actions or what was happening between them, she wouldn't embarrass herself by discussing her strategy with him, but she wasn't about to get hurt again. She was going to stop them from making any more mistakes.

When she entered the kitchen, she saw that Cody had arrived and Chas had set Taylor and Cody in high chairs and was preparing their breakfast cereal.

"How can I help?" she asked pleasantly as she fastened Annie in her high chair beside her brother and sister.

He turned, smiled. "You take Taylor, I'll take Cody, and we'll put Annie in the middle."

"Okay."

Once they began feeding the children, conversation between them became nonexistent because they spoke with the kids. Since Cody was moody and withdrawn this morning, Lily eventually was left to her own devices with both girls. Annie and Taylor had already formed a bond of friendship. They frequently put their heads together and giggled as if sharing a secret, but this morning they appeared to be comparing breakfasts. Annie seemed fascinated by Taylor's cereal, and Taylor seemed equally curious about the oatmeal in Annie's dish. It took only one second of Lily having her back turned for the girls to dip their hands into each other's bowls.

"Taylor! Annie!" Lily gasped. They were giggling with glee as they squashed the gooey cereal between their fingers.

Jumping from his seat, Chas groaned. "Sorry about that."

"It's not your fault," Lily said, hastening to slide the bowls out of the girls' reach and scrubbing cereal from Taylor's fingers with the ever-present wet cloth.

"No, I shouldn't have let you fend for yourself with Annie," he said, as he retrieved another wet cloth.

Cody squealed.

"Actually, this is your fault," Chas said to Cody. "What's the matter with you this morning, anyway?" he asked teasingly, but the baby's face puckered as if he were in pain, and he began to wail loudly.

"Oh, boy!" Lily said, making short order of Taylor's fingers and rushing to grab Cody. After releasing the locks on his high chair, she lifted him into her arms. "What's the matter, honey?" she crooned, but Cody only cried all the harder.

As he wiped Annie's sticky fingers, Chas said, "Let me take him." He took the little boy from Lily's arms, nestled him against his shoulder and began to walk with him. "I'm sorry, buddy," he apologized softly. "I was only teasing."

Cody sniffed and sobbed, wiping his wet nose on the collar of Chas's yellow shirt. Lily turned back to the girls, ready to tackle that disaster, but before she could even reach for their oatmeal bowls, the girls, who had been staring at Cody in bewilderment, glanced at each other and began to cry.

"You know," Chas said, as if he didn't hear his screaming sisters. "I think Cody has a fever."

Not quite sure which child to attend to first, Lily peered at Chas. "Have you ever been around the kids when they were sick?"

"We've cut teeth with them."

"Was this how Cody behaved?" she asked hopefully.

Chas shook his head. "No. When they cut teeth, he seemed more like he was mad than sick. Today, he's more listless, more pitiful," he said, then rubbed his cheek against Cody's warm forehead. "This is something different."

"Take him upstairs," Lily instructed, even as the girls cried. "But not to the nursery. Is there any way we can get a crib into another room?"

Chas only looked at her. "Why?"

"Even if he has something contagious, like a cold, he hasn't been here for twelve hours. There's a chance the girls might not have it."

Chas nodded and started out of the room.

"Take the portable phone with you and call their pediatrician," Lily added, then tossed the phone to Chas.

"Right," he said, caught the phone with one hand and left the room.

"Well, ladies," Lily said to the sobbing baby girls as she removed their oatmeal bowls. "First we're going to check both of you to see if either has a fever, then we're going to make new cereal."

Pounding their high chair trays, both girls continued to cry.

"I'm going to need some help here," she said, looking toward the ceiling, seeking guidance.

Unfortunately, guidance didn't come. In fact, within a half hour it became apparent that Annie also had a fever and Taylor's cheeks were pinkening. Chas phoned Claire and Evan, and they rushed to the house to assist with getting the triplets to the doctor.

Even with four adults and three babies, the situation was difficult at best. While they waited their turn at the pediatrician's office, the children went from one adult to the next, apparently pursuing comfort they couldn't find. Finally the nurse called their names, all four adults crammed into the exam room with the three babies, and after forty-five minutes and a quick blood test, the doctor informed them that the triplets had the flu.

He prescribed some medicines that wouldn't cure the kids, but would help alleviate their symptoms, and as Chas, Evan and Lily were sliding the children into their jackets, Dr. Raymond said, "Your stepmother was really quite a woman. She and your father made wonderful parents. When I heard they'd died, I worried about what would happen with the triplets, but I suppose I should have realized Norm's sons would be excellent caregivers."

Ready to leave, Dr. Raymond shook Evan's hand, then Chas's. "I'm glad to see everything worked out well for the triplets."

For the first ten seconds after he left the exam room, everyone was quiet. Lily had only ever discussed Norm Brewster with Chas, but she knew his marriage had been a bone of contention for the Brewster boys. She knew there were problems and unanswered questions. Feeling the tension around her, she realized the doctor's comments had made both Chas and Evan uncomfortable.

But when everyone was ready to leave, Evan smiled broadly and said, "Well, it looks like Claire and I aren't going back to work today." He paused and faced Chas. "Where's Grant?"

"Savannah," Chas replied with a grimace.

"Once we get the kids to the house, either Claire or I will go home and pack a bag. Even as competent as you appear to be," he said to Lily. "I don't think you guys can handle this alone."

Lily couldn't have agreed more, not just because of the three sick kids, but also because something had happened with Chas. First he liked her, then he kissed her and didn't like her. Then last night he seemed to like her again. And today he kept giving her a ridiculous grin. All in all, he was driving her nuts.

A little company, a little interference, maybe even a little chaperoning was definitely a good thing. Having such strong feelings for Chas had to be a mistake, and if she followed her emotions she chanced getting hurt. More than that, though, Chas would also get hurt. She didn't know what he was thinking by giving her those odd looks and sidelong glances, but he couldn't be thinking clearly.

Through the course of the day, Lily made the best of having Claire and Evan at the house not only in caring for the kids and staying away from Chas, but also in getting to know Claire. Leaving the men to read in the nursery while the children napped that afternoon, Claire and Lily made dinner. After dinner they washed the dishes. And when the kitchen was clean and it appeared the men needed a break from the kids, she and Claire volunteered to get the triplets ready for bed.

When Lily finally got to go to her room, she did so with a clear conscience. She'd done more than her fair share for the babies, and she'd stayed away from Chas without being obvious. She closed her eyes and tried to sleep, but an unexpected sense of doubt crept up on her.

If it was such a good thing that she'd stayed away from him, why did she feel so lonely?

Chas stumbled down to breakfast around nine o'clock the next morning. He hadn't showered or shaved. He was tired, drowning in legal work and handling the lion's share of the responsibility for the triplets. He figured he had every right in the world to take it easy.

Besides, Lily didn't like him, anyway. What the hell was the point?

"Good morning, Chas," Evan said, glancing up from reading the morning paper.

Chas growled an unintelligible response. As far as he was concerned it wasn't a good morning. The triplets were still sick, he had a mountain of paperwork to do, and he was all alone in the world. He trudged to the round table in the breakfast nook. As he sat, he squinted from the brightness of the sunlight streaming in through the horizontal blinds.

"Morning, Chas," Claire said cheerfully.

Though Chas could ignore his brother, he knew it would be rude not to muster a reasonable response for his new sister-in-law and mumbled, "Morning."

A cup of coffee appeared on the table, then Lily softly said, "I made pancakes, if you're interested."

Something akin to a firestorm went through him. Heat seemed to spark from every one of his nerve endings. He tingled in places he didn't know a man could tingle. He didn't need to peer behind him to see what she was wearing. Her voice alone melted him like butter. He never would have thought that the mere sound of a woman's voice could do this kind of damage to a man, but, then again, he knew what the woman looked like who belonged to that voice. He knew how she smelled. He knew how it felt to hold her in his arms. He knew what she tasted like.

He swallowed.

"Or, if you like, you can just have coffee," Lily offered when he didn't answer.

He cleared his throat. "A pancake would be good," he said quietly.

A part of him knew he was making a blasted fool of himself by pouting over the fact that she could so easily avoid him. Another part didn't care. He liked Lily. He really liked her. He wasn't foolhardy enough to call what he felt for her love. He wasn't sure "love" existed. But he did know that his emotions ran much deeper than anything he'd felt for either of the women he'd married.

The question was, what the hell was he supposed to do about it? Not only did she appear uninterested in a relationship because of her recent breakup, but she also didn't appear interested in *him,* period.

It was the kind of blow an ego shouldn't have to suffer.

"Yeah, a pancake would be good," he repeated, staring at his coffee mug.

"Okay," Lily said sweetly.

"I'm through with my breakfast. You sit, Lily," Evan said, rising. "I'll help Chas."

Once again, Chas got a tingling sensation. But this one had nothing to do with his attraction to Lily, and everything to do with Evan making him feel like an idiot for forcing Lily to wait on him. He drained his mug of coffee and pushed away from the table before Evan could get to the stove. "I can make my own," he said. Lord knows he never expected anyone to wait on him. He'd been taking care of himself since college and doing a damned fine job.

"So what are we going to do today?" Evan asked Claire as Chas poured pancake batter onto the griddle.

"Well, we're going to need more clothes than we brought," Claire replied. "And also one of us should go into the office to handle any crises our secretary, Janelle, may have on her hands."

"Hum, you're right," Evan agreed. "Janelle's a trooper and can pretty much handle anything, but because she's so worried about the triplets, I think she'd try to keep any real crisis from us."

"So, do you want to go or do you want me to go?" Claire asked.

Chas flipped his pancake, then rubbed his hand across the back of his neck, feeling guilty for getting mad at Evan for making him look bad. Everybody had too much work to do. Everybody was taking responsibility for the triplets. Evan hadn't been trying to make him look bad earlier, he was simply attempting to get everything done and to keep the workload as even as possible.

"I think you should go," Evan said. "Not only can

you choose better clothes for both of us, but I think you can use a few minutes away from the triplets.''

Getting a pang of irritation again, Chas stopped fiddling with his pancake and unwittingly gave the conversation his complete attention.

"And take Lily with you," Evan added. "A little fresh air and sunshine will do you both a lot of good."

Chas turned and gaped at his brother. There was no call for that kind of generosity. Now there would only be two of them to care for three very sick kids. But worse, since he'd hired Lily he'd never even thought to give her time off. The only furlough she got was the afternoon *she'd* requested. Intentional or not, his brother had just made him look stupid.

Chas was on the brink of getting furious with Evan, when Claire bounced from her seat, planted a wonderful kiss on Evan's lips, and said, "Thanks. I love you. And I owe you one. Come on, Lily."

Looking a little surprised, but also grateful, Lily quickly scrambled from her seat. "Let me grab a jacket," she said, "And I'll be right behind you."

In that second Chas knew Evan hadn't done any of that to make Chas look bad but to make Evan look good. He knew the value of the gesture was worth far more than the price of caring for the triplets alone this morning, particularly considering that they were actually sleeping more than anything else.

Okay. So, his brother was a pretty smart guy.

Unfortunately, the repercussion was that he'd also inadvertently made Chas look bad.

After a quick trip to Evan and Claire's apartment, Claire and Lily jumped into Claire's sport utility vehicle.

"This is really a terrific SUV."

Claire laughed. "Thanks, but it's Evan's. He's had it a while, I think."

Lily glanced around at the sophisticated leather interior, then thought of the feminine touches still lingering in Claire's apartment and she said, "You two didn't know each other long, did you?"

"Not really," Claire admitted, turning the vehicle up Main Street. "We met for the first time about an hour after his father's funeral last May." She paused, casting a quick glance at Lily. "I had worked for Evan's father for a little over a year as his assistant. Loved the man. I saw many of his good traits in Evan. So when I fell it was quick and it was hard. Do you mind if we stop at the diner?"

"No. Not at all."

"Good. I haven't checked on Abby since before we came out to stay with you and the kids, and the last time we talked she was having a little trouble with Tyler."

Lily remembered the bright-eyed little boy. "I can't imagine Tyler giving anyone trouble."

"Well, it's not real trouble," Claire said, parking the sport utility vehicle in front of the diner. "It's more that Abby's afraid he's going to start asking about his father."

Confused, Lily didn't say anything as she and Claire got out of the SUV.

"Since you're going to be in on the conversation," Claire said, walking beside Lily toward the diner. "I guess I'd better explain that Abby never married Tyler's father. She also never told Tyler anything about his dad because it's something of a touchy subject for her, and because Tyler never asked. Now so much time has passed that Abby's not sure how to handle the situation."

"I read that you're not supposed to tell kids about sex until they question you, because if the topic hasn't come up for them, then they're not mature enough to understand it. When they ask, they're ready to know," Lily said, motioning for Claire to precede her into the entryway. "Maybe Abby should just use that same philosophy."

Claire stopped before pushing open the diner door, and faced Lily. "Maybe she should." She smiled warmly. "I'm glad I brought you."

"So am I," Lily replied, laughing as she and Claire entered the diner. "I couldn't have handled another day with three sick kids and no break."

Though one or two patrons still sat at the counter nursing cups of coffee, the bulk of the breakfast crowd was gone, and all of the booths were empty.

"Anybody home?" Claire called, stripping off her rust-colored suede coat.

Abby came bustling out of the kitchen. When she saw Claire, she deflated as if she'd been ready to reprimand the miscreant who'd dared yell in her restaurant. But she wouldn't scold Claire because she'd been teasing. As if to get her bearings, she shook her head, causing her mane of red hair to brush across her back. "Hi."

"Hi," Claire said, smiling devilishly. "You remember Lily," she added.

"Yeah, I've met Lily twice," Abby said, watching Lily and Claire slide onto stools at the counter. "Once at the B&B and once when she was here for pie."

"Well, you should have protected her from predators. While you were adding the ice cream to that pie, Arnie Garrett ran her through the third degree."

Abby grimaced. "Sorry. I didn't see that."

"It's okay," Lily replied, sighing. "I didn't tell him

SUSAN MEIER   105

too much, and Chas is sure what I did say wasn't worth anything.''

Obviously picking up on something in Lily's voice, Claire and Abby exchanged a look.

"How are things with you and Chas?" Claire asked, bracing her elbow on the counter and her chin on her closed fist.

Lily felt herself color uncontrollably. "What do you mean?"

"I mean, we've always heard he was quite a ladies' man," Abby said, leaning down to place her elbow beside Claire's so the two women could interrogate Lily. "Has he tried to kiss you yet?"

This time Lily felt all the blood drain from her face.

Claire gasped. "He has!"

Abby gave her friend a shocked look. "What are you gasping for? Staying alone in that house with those babies is what brought you and Evan together."

"Evan and I were working together. We would have found each other one way or another," Claire said, unfazed.

"Yeah, maybe," Abby agreed skeptically. "But there's something strange or mysterious about those kids. Or maybe magical," she added whimsically.

"What do you mean?" Lily asked, eager to change the subject.

"Well, I'm not really sure why Norm and Angela got married," Abby said. "But the rumor I heard was they were planning to split up when Angela discovered she was pregnant."

Claire reluctantly nodded her consensus.

"So the kids kept them together," Abby added.

"Do you think Angela married Norm for his money?" Lily asked.

Claire shook her head. "No. She couldn't have. There was a prenuptial agreement as thick as the Bible."

"So what was the deal?" Lily asked.

Claire shrugged. "Norm never said a word to me, except that he dearly loved the babies and he was glad he'd remarried."

Abby shook her head. "Any news I got came after the marriage. I never heard a word about their beginnings."

"It's just all so odd," Lily said. "Every day I see three grown men with three baby siblings, and, just like you, Abby, I know there's something more here than meets the eye."

"Everybody says so," Abby concurred. "And most people think the secret lies with Angela." Tongue in cheek, Abby added, "Maybe she was left at the altar and married Norm on the rebound."

Lily laughed. "You're making a joke, but I wouldn't be surprised. Getting left at the altar leaves you with some really strange feelings."

"Is that why you kissed Chas?" Claire asked, her eyebrows raised in question.

"I didn't kiss Chas."

"That's right," Abby agreed. "He kissed you. And you somehow avoided giving us details."

"Because there aren't any details to give," Lily said shyly.

Obviously done teasing, Claire said, "I'll tell you what, Lily. Chas is a really nice guy, but at this point he's still got some issues to work out in his life. If it were me and I didn't want to get hurt again, I think I'd keep my distance."

"I am," Lily agreed quietly.

Abby crossed her arms on her chest and turned as

somber as Claire had. "It isn't that Chas isn't a good guy. He is."

"He's a wonderful guy. A really sweet guy," Claire agreed.

"But..." Lily said when both women fell silent.

"But you're an extremely beautiful woman, Lily. You could be on the cover of a fashion magazine. And Chas has got a thing for really pretty women," Claire said with a sigh.

Abby disagreed with a shake of her head. "No. I think that's only the tip of the iceberg. The truth is that all men have a thing for really pretty women, but most men know their limits."

Lily frowned. "What's that supposed to mean?"

Abby said simply, "Grant has always been the big, strong, tough Brewster. Evan has always been the smart, conservative, decisive Brewster. And Chas, well, Chas has always been the frivolous, devilish, spoiled Brewster."

"Are you telling me that's how he defines himself?" Lily asked dubiously.

Abby shook her head. "No, I'm telling you that no one's ever told him no. He doesn't know how to handle no. His mother spoiled him. His father spoiled him. Every time he got into trouble his older brothers bailed him out. And if a woman dumped him, there was always another to take her place."

"I never looked at it that way," Claire said thoughtfully.

"Well, think about it," Abby said. "Why would he marry one woman after another without regard for consequences except if he couldn't stand the thought of losing?"

After a few moments the conversation turned to Tyler.

Abby happily announced that her son hadn't asked one word about his father, but now that she knew the possibility existed, she would give some real thought to how she should answer him.

They laughed and teased a bit more about Claire's quick courtship and marriage to Evan, and when it was time to go, Claire and Lily were laughing as they exited the diner.

But Abby's comments about Chas echoed in Lily's head the whole drive home. She didn't necessarily buy the idea that Chas was spoiled, but she could see that he didn't like to lose. It was a very simple, very obvious explanation for why he'd be disinterested one day and begin to pursue her two days later—after she rejected him.

She could resist his honeyed compliments, innuendos and even searing glances over bologna sandwiches, but she explicitly recalled that his last kiss had been pure sweetness and raw emotion. Beautiful, wonderful, dangerous things to a woman who'd gone far too long without affection.

If he kissed her again, he would see her weakness wasn't for sex, she hadn't fallen for his charm, and she didn't care about his commanding presence. No, he would see quite clearly that she was a sucker for a really good kiss, a romantic gesture, and even as little as a drop of affection.

And then there would be no turning back. She would get hurt. He would hurt her because he didn't really care for her. He just didn't like to lose.

So why was it she found herself wishing he would make one more try at sweeping her off her feet?

Chapter Eight

When Claire and Lily returned with bags of takeout they'd bought at the diner, Chas knew his brother was probably close to a genius. They'd not only brought lunch, but both Claire and Lily were relaxed and happy. Evan was even rewarded with another long, lingering kiss that held the kind of potential and promises Chas could only dream about.

He glanced at Lily and saw that she was studying Evan and Claire with an undisguised look of longing. He knew women liked the schmaltzy things Evan always did, but somehow or other it all seemed contrived, fake, almost like cheating. Not that he thought Evan cheated Claire. He knew from Evan's romantic heart that gestures like this were natural for him. Especially with Claire. Chas had never seen any man who loved a woman the way Evan loved Claire. And the way Evan loved Claire seemed to make Claire love him as much in return.

Even though the system suddenly became crystal

clear, and even though Chas was fairly certain he could trick Lily into seeing him differently if he'd imitate Evan, Chas concluded he couldn't do it because the important word was *trick*. He'd never won a woman through trickery before. He'd never had to. Not only was it dishonest, but it seemed disloyal to himself, almost as if he were conceding defeat or admitting to a problem. And he didn't have a problem. All women loved him.

Unfortunately, even as he watched Lily run up the steps in her perfect jeans, with her blond hair bouncing around her, his libido begged to differ.

Later that afternoon, Chas found Lily alone in the kitchen. When he observed her odd expression upon seeing him enter, he almost turned around and gave her her privacy, but he recognized that they couldn't live together in the same house and have her constantly running away from him. Somehow, he had to let her know that there were no hard feelings because of her rejection and that he could treat her perfectly normally, like a friend—until he figured out a way to seduce her fairly.

"Hey," he said, entering the room.

"Hey," she replied, her eyes fixed on the recipe she was reading.

"Where's Claire?"

"She and Evan are outside, taking a walk."

He heard the wistful quality in her voice and almost sighed. Taking a walk was another one of those mushy, romantic things Evan liked to do, and one of those damned romantic things women swooned over. One of those things that might make Lily change the way she felt about him.

But once again Chas reminded himself he couldn't be Evan. He wasn't built that way. His relationships were usually mutual. He'd never chased a woman in his life.

Besides, it would be cheating, and he wouldn't cheat Lily. He'd already figured all this out.

"What are you doing?"

She shrugged. "Looking for recipes. I thought while we had help with the kids, I'd try to find a recipe for something unusual, but easy, that we could use when we're alone again."

The last part of her sentence hung in the air between them. Because of the way he'd kissed her the last time they were alone, he knew that unless he said something consoling, pacifying or borderline repentant now, when Evan and Claire left she would be as nervous as a cat in a room full of rocking chairs.

"Maybe Grant will get home before Claire and Evan have to leave?" he suggested, subtly trying to alleviate her fears, but a spark of irritation rose before he could squelch it. He hated tiptoeing around his feelings. He wasn't an animal, for Pete's sake. True, he was attracted to her, but he would never take advantage of her. He'd never taken advantage of any woman. He'd never had to.

"I'm not afraid of you."

"Really?" he asked, not even bothering to hide his skepticism.

"Really," she said, as if exasperated. "If anything, I'm annoyed with myself because I don't understand what's going on between us."

"I can tell you what's going on between us," Chas said, busying himself with getting some grapes from the fruit bowl in the center of the table so he didn't have to look at her. "I'm attracted to you, and—"

He paused and glanced at her. For weeks he'd been getting mixed signals, and even though she'd straight-forwardly rejected him, he refused to discount the good things he'd seen just because of one little rejection. One rejection up against at least four dreamy-eyed stares and two good kisses didn't stack up.

That was the inconsistency that had been bugging him for days. Her rejection didn't add up. It didn't make a damned whit of sense.

"I don't have a problem following through on my attraction," he continued, catching her gaze. "And you're attracted to me, but you can't follow through."

She studied him for several long minutes, obviously considering her answer carefully. Chas figured that if she truly didn't like him at all, she wouldn't have to think about it. Since she was thinking, she felt something between them.

She sighed. "You're right."

It wasn't an admission of undying love, but for Chas's battered ego, it was like a bouquet of sonnets. He didn't need fancy words. He didn't need strong declarations. He didn't really need anything, but just her being willing to admit she found him attractive boosted his spirits.

"So, we'll just cool it for a while," he said casually, shifting his attention to the grapes again. "Give both of our lives a chance to settle down."

She returned her focus to the recipe book. "That would be a good idea."

"Good," he echoed, confirming everything so there would be no misunderstanding. In that second, the sun seemed brighter, the world seemed calmer, and life seemed like a fun place again. He could breathe. He could think. Hell, now that he knew she found him attractive and probably even liked him, he actually believed he could go back into the den and work again.

When Evan and Claire came running into the kitchen

from the back door, laughing, holding hands, Chas saw them in a completely different light.

Maybe they weren't half as schmaltzy as he'd thought they were.

Lily was very glad she and Chas had had their short but important conversation that afternoon because the next morning the triplets showed marked improvement. They gave the kids one more day to be sure they really were recovered, and after bathtime that night the four caregivers pronounced them healthy.

Evan and Claire decided to go to bed early since they'd not only have to go to work the next morning, they'd have to wake in time to go to their apartment for appropriate work clothes. Because of that, Lily and Chas were left to their own devices after nine o'clock.

She knew she easily could have made the same kind of excuse as Evan and Claire and slipped off to her room, but she not only didn't want to upset Chas again, now that they'd more or less straightened things out between them, but also she didn't feel like being alone.

"Cards?"

Lily glanced over at Chas and grimaced. "I don't think so."

"Why not?"

"Because I don't know all those stupid rules and exceptions and I'm not in the mood to make a fool of myself."

"Come on, take the plunge," Chas said, urging her to the round card table in the family room. "I made a damned fool of myself many times and I lived. Proof positive you'll live if you make a fool of yourself tonight. Besides, I'm willing to forgo all those stupid rules and exceptions, in order to alleviate the boredom."

Under those conditions, Lily agreed. "Okay. You deal."

He flashed her a grin. "Every hand if you like."

They played three rounds of rummy in near silence with Lily concentrating so hard she didn't have the mental energy left to hold a conversation. After the fourth hand Chas whistled. "What did you do, practice?"

She laughed with the delight at a job well done. "No. But Claire and I played a game or two last night."

Chas leaned back and studied her. "Trying to impress me?"

She felt her cheeks redden. "No."

"Then why'd you do it?"

"Because I don't like to look stupid."

Continuing to regard her, he considered that for another moment, then said, "You're one of the most careful, cautious people I know. I can't picture you ever having done anything stupid."

"You should have seen me when I was younger."

Bracing his elbow on the card table, Chas grinned. "I would have liked to have seen you when you were younger."

From the expression on his face, Lily believed him. But she also realized he had some sort of idealized image of her, which actually fit in with what Abby had speculated about him at the diner. He not only didn't like to hear the word *no*, but he also had a thing for pretty girls.

She sighed heavily. For Lily it felt like a moment of truth. He was attracted to her. She was attracted to him. From the way they kissed, neither one of them could lie about it. But the truth of the matter was she didn't want to be involved in another relationship that was going nowhere. Since Abby and Claire seemed to believe Chas was a man who couldn't take no for an answer, Lily didn't want to tell him no only to have him become more determined. So she wasn't going to put them in that position. Instead, she was going to tell him the absolute, bottom-line truth about herself. Once he found out she wasn't perfect, he wouldn't want her anymore, and they could get on with the rest of their lives.

"Trust me. You wouldn't have wanted to have seen me when I was younger," she told Chas quietly. "I was stupid and I was pigheaded. But I cleaned up my act pretty quickly because my parents were killed in an automobile accident when I was sixteen."

"I'm sorry."

Lily shook her head. "I didn't have to live in foster care or anything. I wasn't alone. I went to live with my sister and her husband almost immediately."

Chas frowned. "*Almost* immediately?"

"I stayed in my parents' house by myself for three weeks, trying to prove to Mary Louise and the rest of the world I could make it on my own."

"Social Services would let you do that?"

Lily laughed. "Probably not, but Mary Louise has a stubborn streak as thick as mine. She knew I needed private grieving time, and somehow she found her way around the red tape and gave it to me."

From the look on his face, Lily could tell he was superimposing his own experiences into the life of a sixteen-year-old and wasn't happy with the results.

He leaned forward on the table. "You stayed all by yourself for three whole weeks?"

Lily nodded. "Telling Mary Louise I could take care of myself, but actually grieving."

"Your sister must be something."

"She is. She and her husband had three kids and troubles enough of their own. They didn't need to be burdened with me, too, but they took me in anyway.''

"And that's why you stayed by yourself? You didn't want to intrude.''

Picking up the cards again, Lily shrugged. "Never have.''

"It's also why you like to make your own way in life.''

Seeing that she definitely wasn't fitting into the mold of the perky little lady he typically dated and married, she nodded, then laughed at the confused expression on his face. "Men do things like this all the time and writers turn their tales into epics. But a woman does one slightly out-of-whack thing and you think there's something wrong with her.''

"I don't think there's anything wrong with you,'' Chas disagreed, but he would privately admit to himself that he was baffled. His two wives and his near miss had all been in their twenties, yet two of them wouldn't have stayed alone anywhere if their lives depended upon it. The third still couldn't support herself, probably never would be able to. But at sixteen Lily had faced one of life's saddest challenges, the loss of her parents, and she'd done it alone.

"My parents had a fairly nice insurance policy so that softened the blow of having to take me in. My sister and her husband used the benefit money to buy a house, and once I got myself under control we all lived somewhat happily for a while.''

Chas waited for her to continue. When she didn't, he said, "Then what happened?''

She shrugged as if the rest of the story was no big deal. "Money got tight, Mary Louise went back to work, and instead of going to college I volunteered to be her live-in baby-sitter.''

"You regret it?''

"Yes and no," Lily replied honestly. "It was almost pointless for my sister to work if she also had to pay a baby-sitter. And they'd done me a huge favor by taking me in.''

"But...''

"But, now I'm a twenty-three-year-old woman with nothing to show for her life.''

"Twenty-three's pretty young to be worried that you don't have anything to show for your life.''

At that Lily smiled, mesmerizing Chas. "At sixteen I turned into an adult. I knew that every forkful of food that went into my mouth was somebody else's provision. My sister and her husband might have gotten a government stipend, but it wasn't enough to compensate for feeding me and putting a roof over my head. From the day my parents died, I have felt I was a burden. For once, I'd like not to be.''

With that she combed her fingers through her long, straight hair. "You know what? I'm a little more tired than I thought I was. I think I'll turn in for the night, too.''

Long after she was gone, Chas stared off into space. When a man saw a woman who looked like Lily, his thoughts turned to ease and luxury. Even he had assumed that she couldn't handle three kids. He'd actually believed she wouldn't want to. But the truth of the matter was, he would bet that Lily would give her last cent to belong. It was why she fit so well into the Brewster family—they needed her. By being needed, she felt wanted. By feeling wanted, she felt acceptable.

He hated the very thought that Lily had spent one day

feeling unloved, unwanted or alone. Not merely because
no human being should ever feel such pain, but because
this was Lily. Good, kind, generous Lily who deserved
much, much better.

A deep, intense emotion flooded him. In a flash of
insight, he realized why Evan catered to Claire and even
why Claire catered to Evan. Caring for someone didn't
make you weak or bewitched. A man didn't even care
for his woman to ensure the continuation of his relationship, or to guarantee his wife's love. He cared for her
because he knew in his heart that his wife deserved
someone to care for her. He cared for her because he
wanted to. Something about her called to something in
him. And if a man was wise, he responded.

Well, Chas decided, he was responding.

If anyone deserved to be catered to and cared for it
was Lily.

He may not want to marry her, and she absolutely,
positively, definitely didn't want to marry him, but unless Chas missed his guess, Lily was long overdue to
have someone care for and comfort her.

The next morning Evan and Claire left without incident.

When they were gone, Chas and Lily flipped a coin
to see who would vacuum the downstairs and who would
do the laundry. Chas lost the toss and carried basket after
basket of dirty baby clothes to the kitchen for sorting,
while Lily happily grabbed the vacuum and predicted
she'd be done quickly enough to run the errands in town.
But before ten o'clock, Chas noticed that Lily's cheeks
had a bright pink hue about them.

"Are you okay?" he asked cautiously.

She smiled weakly. "Yeah. I'm fine."

"Why don't you let me go into town to restock the medicine cabinet?"

Lily laughed. "Not on your life. I won that coin toss fair and square. I'm *not* doing the laundry."

"Okay, I'll tell you what," Chas suggested. "If you let me go into town, you can save the laundry for when I get home."

She narrowed her eyes suspiciously. "Why are you so anxious to go into town?"

"I'm not," he immediately denied. "I'm trying to save you from going into town because you don't look good."

"I'm fine," she insisted, but Chas noticed that she sort of swooned, catching herself with a quick hand to the corner of the kitchen countertop.

"You're not fine," he said, striding over to her. He placed his palm on her forehead, and just as he suspected, her skin felt feverish. He sighed. "Great. You caught the flu about three hours too late."

"I didn't know we were on a schedule," she said groggily.

"We're not, but we've lost Evan and Claire." He paused and thought about that. "I'll just call them and ask them to come back," he said, and turned her around to lead her through the kitchen and the adjoining alcove into her bedroom.

When Lily only sat on the bed, Chas sighed. "Do you need help changing into pajamas?"

"No."

"Then strip and put on a nightgown or something and climb into bed or I'll do it for you."

Lily gave him an annoyed frown, but Chas only glanced at his watch. "It's 10:15. I'll be back in five minutes,'' he said, walking to the door. "If I were you I wouldn't waste any time."

In the kitchen he picked up the phone to dial the number for the lumber mill, ready to ask Evan and Claire to return, but before he got to the sixth digit, he stopped himself.

The night before, he'd decided he wanted a chance to pamper and care for Lily, and fate had handed him the perfect opportunity on a silver platter. He needed to revive her opinion of him, but more than that he knew she needed to see that someone would go out of his way to take care of her. Since she wouldn't let anyone care for her when she was well, and since he suspected she'd bite off his hand if he tried to pamper her, her getting sick was the best thing that could have happened to them.

At 10:20, he walked into her room and discovered she was sound asleep. Breathing a sigh of relief, he closed the vertical blinds on her window, bringing the room into complete darkness. He tiptoed to the door and softly closed it behind him.

This would be fun.

Chapter Nine

Chas walked out of Lily's bedroom and, through the monitor, heard the sound of at least two of the babies crying. Reminding himself he'd handled the kids by himself before, he jogged up the steps and into the nursery.

Annie was sitting up in her crib, sobbing pitifully. Big, wet tears streamed down her cherubic cheeks. Angry, Cody stood clinging to the bars of his crib and wailed. A strong little boy, Cody could not only balance himself enough to stand, but he could also shake the bars and rattle his crib. Through it all, Taylor slept peacefully.

Okay. No problem. Anybody could handle two kids without help.

Since Cody was mad, but Annie was sad, Chas reached for Annie first. "What's the matter, little one?" he crooned.

Giving her reply in baby talk, Annie spit all over him, then rubbed her wet nose in his shirt.

"I don't blame you for being upset," Chas said,

checking her diaper. "I don't think I'd like having wet pants, either."

Cody squealed.

"Shhh!" Chas said, putting a finger to his lips as he took Annie to the changing table. "You can't be doing this kind of stuff today. Lily is sick. Evan and Claire have gone home. So it's just me."

Cody obviously couldn't have cared less for Chas's troubles. Otherwise, he wouldn't have let out with a bloodcurdling scream.

"I'm telling you, you're gonna wake—"

Before Chas could say her name, Taylor stirred. Because she'd been roused before she got sufficient rest, she had to work to pry her little eyes opened. But also because she'd been awakened before she wanted to be, she wasn't precisely happy about it. Chas watched her eyes pool with tears, her face pucker and her little lips turn downward into a mad scowl. Within two seconds, she was screaming with Cody.

"Guys, this isn't going to work," Chas singsonged, making short order of Annie's diaper and carefully placing her in the play yard. He reached for Cody. "You can't do this today."

In response to the patient suggestion, Cody screeched, rolled his fingers into a fist and punched Chas's cheek when he scooped him out of the crib.

Chas narrowed his eyes. "You're lucky you're shorter than I am."

Using the railing of her crib for leverage, Taylor pulled herself to her feet, screaming at the top of her lungs. Even as Chas worked on Cody, Annie peered at her sister as if analyzing her situation and then decided to join in on the crying. Chas couldn't tell if it was sympathy crying, fear-based crying or just plain joining in because it seemed like the thing to do, but he now had a symphony of noise surrounding him.

"All right, that's enough," he shouted, but no one paid any attention, so he took a deep breath, counted to ten and reminded himself that this, too, would pass.

And when it had passed he would have Lily all to himself again. Sure, she was sick. And, yes, her being sick wasn't what anybody would call an ideally romantic situation. But it was the environment he needed to pamper her. So if that meant he had to put up with caring for three babies alone, that's what he would do.

He soothed the kids enough that he could carry them downstairs and settle them in the kitchen while he prepared their lunch. With them seated in the high chairs and their dinners warming, he drew a long breath and concluded he should take advantage of this free minute to toss a load of laundry into the washer. He set the dial and started the water flowing into the tub, but before he got even half of a load of baby clothes piled inside, one of the kids screamed.

Taylor! Damn, he wished the other two had let her sleep.

"I'm coming," he called, his voice barely above a whisper because the laundry room was on the other side of the alcove in front of Lily's room. He rushed into the kitchen, quieted Taylor and realized that he'd have to set things up better if he wanted to get anything done today. With that in mind, he kicked the baskets filled with laundry toward the alcove, stacking them in front of Lily's door. The microwave bell sounded at the same minute he heard the squeak of springs, indicating Lily had risen from her bed.

He wasn't going to let her help him. *No way,* he thought, jumping over the baskets to get to the kitchen, but he didn't jump high enough and one basket of dirty baby sleepers poured out onto the kitchen floor.

No big deal. He'd get it once the kids were fed.

Rushing to the microwave, he wondered why Lily hadn't appeared from the bedroom yet. He divided the warmed baby food among the three little plates in front of him and frowned. He knew he'd heard the bed squeak.

Cody yelped. Annie squealed. Taylor began to cry in earnest.

Chas scratched the back of his neck, figuring Lily must have gotten up to go to the bathroom or something. He took the three plates of food to the high chairs, issuing soothing words to get everyone to calm down, and eventually he fed all three kids. But before it was all over he was wearing more mashed carrots on his shirt than the kids had in their stomachs. He gave them each a cookie to compensate for the calorie loss and had just pulled Taylor out of her high chair when the doorbell rang.

Great! Who could that be?

Carrying Taylor, he ran to the door and opened it. Mrs. Pawlowski stared at him.

"Good morning, Mr. Brewster," she said with a pleasantness that didn't quite reach her eyes.

"Mrs. Pawlowski, did we have an appointment?"

"We had a hearing," she said, smiling a smile that was strained from the effort of trying to be understanding. "Twenty minutes ago. The judge tried to call you."

"Ah, damn!" Chas said, motioning her inside. "I'll call the judge right now and ask for a continuance."

"If you mean that the hearing can be held later, Judge Flenner said it's no problem," the woman said, declining his invitation to come inside with a shake of her head, even as she frowned at the splattering of smashed carrots on his shirt. "I have to go to work, but you still might want to call the judge. He was pretty mad that you had no respect for his time."

"*His* time?" Chas said, with a groan.

"Are you having a problem, Mr. Brewster?" Ginny Pawlowski asked carefully.

"No. No, everything's fine," he lied in a low, tight voice, because even though everything wasn't precisely fine, there was nothing Ginny Pawlowski could do about it. "Don't worry, I'll call the judge."

Chas closed the door on Mrs. Pawlowski and put Taylor in the play yard in the family room, then ran to the kitchen to get Cody and Annie. Unfortunately, he'd forgotten to take their empty dishes from the high chair trays, and Annie was wearing hers on her head like a hat. Cody had carrots on his nose.

"All right, guys," Chas said, holding back another groan. He picked up the wet cloth from the table, but heard something fall in Lily's room. Dropping the cloth, he ran to see what it was. When he opened the door, it bumped against a vase, but it was lightweight and he could still push the door open far enough to gain access to the room. When he stepped inside, he put his foot in a puddle of water spilled from the vase.

"Damn it!" he yelped, yanking his foot back, but it was too late. His sock was soaked.

Not seeing Lily in her bed, he forgot all about his sock and swallowed his panic. "Lily?"

She didn't say anything, but he heard awful retching noises from her bathroom. Scrubbing his hand down his face, Chas considered that she probably didn't need company, but when he heard her groan, he ran in to see what was going on.

Pushing open the bathroom door just a fraction, only

enough to peek inside, he saw Lily was lying on the floor.

"Oh, my God," he said, scrambling to her side. "Lily," he said, sliding his arm under her shoulders to lift her head.

"I'm okay."

"My God. You're not okay! Otherwise, you wouldn't be lying on the floor."

"It's cool down here."

"Yeah, right," he said, realizing she was burning up with fever. "We're going to have to get some aspirin in you or something," he said, rising to go to the medicine cabinet.

"Just get me a cool cloth for my head and go take care of the kids."

"Let me help you back to bed," Chas said, as he grabbed a cloth from the shelf behind the door and wet it.

Lily moaned pitifully. "I think I need to stay right here."

"I don't like leaving you," Chas argued.

The sound of a plate breaking in the kitchen caught Chas's attention and raised Lily's head. "Go," she insisted.

"Right," Chas agreed and scampered off, but he just didn't feel okay about leaving Lily. He scrubbed everybody's face clean, soaked up the water from the vase Lily had dropped on her way to the bathroom and took all three kids into her bedroom.

When Claire found them twenty minutes later, the kids were crawling through the spilled laundry, Lily was leaning over the sink and Chas was holding her hair off her face.

"I don't know why you're here, but I'm thanking God right now."

Reaching for Annie, Claire clucked her tongue. "Mrs. Pawlowski called me," she said, looking at the carrot stains on Chas's shirt. "And I'm glad she did. Why didn't *you* call?"

"There wasn't time," Chas explained, but Lily cut him off.

Turning to look at Claire, she sighed heavily. "Oh, God, am I glad to see you. The kids are all over the place. The house is a mess. *I* feel terrible," she said as Claire bundled her robe around her and directed her to her bed again.

"Caught the flu, did you?" Claire joked as she led Lily to her bed.

"My head hurts so much, I can't even think," Lily said, sliding into bed again. "You'll stay?"

"Of course I'll stay. And Evan will be here just as soon as he is done at the lumber mill."

"Good," Lily said, snuggling against her pillow.

Chas leaned against the door frame of the bathroom. Confusion warred with anger in his belly. If he didn't know better he'd think Lily didn't regard him as being capable of caring for her...or the triplets. In fact, all politeness and consideration aside, he knew damned well she didn't consider him capable of caring for the triplets. Never mind thinking him capable of caring for her.

When Lily awakened feeling much better two days later, she was awash with regret. It wasn't so much that she hadn't done her duties, but Chas had not only taken up the lion's share of the work, he'd pampered her.

She squeezed her eyes shut. Lord, he'd held her hair back while she lost her breakfast.

Combing her fingers through that same hair, which hadn't seen water in forty-eight hours, Lily had absolutely no idea what to make of that. She took a shower, dried and styled her hair, dressed in real clothes for the first time in days and felt as good as new.

Her first thought was to thank Chas, but when she stepped into the family room and saw that not only Claire and Evan, but also Grant had joined the family, she didn't feel comfortable thanking Chas for holding her hair out of the way while she was in one of life's most embarrassing positions. She settled for saying, "Hi."

"Hey, look who's up," Grant said, bounding from the sofa, Cody on his arm. "How are you feeling?"

"Judging from the fact that she's dressed, I'd say she's fine," Claire said.

"I am fine," she said, smiling. "And I'm sorry. I'll catch up with all the work I missed."

"You'll do no such thing," Evan insisted. "You'll rest for another day before you do anything. In fact, you look like you could use some food."

"No, thanks, I think I'll pass for now. Maybe I'll have some toast in a couple of hours," Lily said.

"Well, the kids need lunch and so do I," Grant said, walking to the door. "You just rest."

"I'll help with the kids," Claire volunteered, rising from her chair.

"Me, too," Evan seconded, and before Lily really knew what was happening, she was alone with Chas.

She felt butterflies in her stomach and pressed her hand there.

"You okay?" he asked immediately, noticing the gesture.

She cleared her throat. "I'm fine. Except I'm embarrassed."

He glanced at her. "Embarrassed?"

"Chas, I know how sick I was. I know you took care of me."

He shrugged. "Until Claire came."

"I just want you to know I appreciate it."

He waited until he caught her gaze, then said, "And I just want you to know it was no big deal. Lily, I like you. People who like each other do things like that for each other."

Lily disagreed with a shake of her head. "No. Holding a woman's hair while she tosses her cookies is above and beyond the call of duty. Only family does things like that."

He gave her a curious look. "You don't think you're family here?"

She hadn't really thought about it, but now that she did she supposed she was. "I guess."

"I know," he insisted and walked over to her. "You are the silliest thing," he said, cupping her chin in his hand and raising her face until she looked at him. "I'm not exactly sure what we have to do to prove to you that we like you, but we like you," he said, then he bent his head and kissed her.

The kiss was long and slow and deep enough for Chas to feel a yearning that stretched the whole way to his toes. But he didn't rush things. First he'd been worried about her. Then he'd been angry with her. Then he'd gone back to being worried again, but he refused to go into her room because she'd insulted him. Now that she was well, and he saw that her reasoning was only as complex as embarrassment, he was so grateful he was willing to take anything he could get.

And right now he was getting a kiss. A long, lingering, delicious kiss. He used his tongue, his teeth and his lips like lethal weapons, forcing her to admit she liked him, too, if only because she couldn't stop herself from responding. He let his hands slide down her back, feeling for himself that she was warm and well, and slid them back up again just because it felt wonderful to do so. Her hands inched along his arms until they met at his neck and she was holding on to him as tightly as he was holding onto her, and Chas felt a surge of elation that nearly overwhelmed him.

Unfortunately, at the same second he heard the sound of Grant clearing his throat. Lily froze and Chas squeezed his eyes shut.

"Claire asked me to come in and see if you'd like some lunch."

Chas cleared his throat. Lily stepped away from him.

"Since you seem to be starving," Grant said in a tight voice seasoned with disappointment, "let me suggest you follow me into the kitchen right now."

Chapter Ten

"Is anybody staying at the bed and breakfast tonight?" Chas asked Abby, as he stood in front of the diner counter, his hands stuffed in the pockets of his jeans.

She blinked and looked up from the newspaper she was reading. "What?"

"You got anybody staying at the bed and breakfast this weekend?"

"No." Her eyes narrowed. "Why?"

"Because I'm desperate for some privacy."

Abby's face lit with a grin. "Kids getting to you?"

Since that was the truth, Chas nodded. "Kids, Claire, Evan and Grant." He scowled. "Especially Grant. I swear, Abby, I just need twenty-four hours by myself."

"By yourself?" Abby questioned, her expression twisting in confusion. "Tyler and I live in that house. What do you want us to do while you get your twenty-four hours of privacy?"

"Don't you have a relative you could visit somewhere?"

She thought about that. "My brother's been asking us to come see his place in New York. We could do that, but..."

"But what?" he asked, sensing the light at the end of the tunnel and refusing to let it slip away.

"But I'm supposed to work this weekend."

"Isn't there someone who could replace you?"

"Well, sure, but I need the money."

He reached into his pocket. "Here's a hundred dollars for twenty-four hours of having the bed and breakfast to myself, and another hundred dollars for you to leave town."

She stared at the money, then at him. "You're kidding?"

"No. I told you. I'm desperate."

"Well, your desperation is my good luck," she said, snatching the money from his fingers. "Because I could use a weekend away. Two hundred dollars buys you the weekend, honey. You can cook, watch TV, have a sleepover if you like. All I ask is that you do your own dishes."

"Done," he said, and grabbed her hand. He pulled her halfway across the counter, then leaned over and pressed a smacking kiss on her cheek. "You're the best."

"No, I'm simply too poor to be proud. And I need the weekend away. So does Tyler."

"Thanks," Chas said, walking out into the cold late-October day. Dark clouds rolled across the sky, and the temperature seemed to be dropping by the minute. But he didn't care. He had a place. Now all he had to do was figure out a way to get Lily to the bed and breakfast.

"She what?"

"She thinks you might have left something at the bed

and breakfast the day you stayed there," Chas said non-chalantly, though inside, his heart was beating fiercely. He hadn't lied in so long he'd forgotten how difficult it was, but he'd told himself that technically this wasn't lying. Lily really may have left something at the bed and breakfast. Abby simply hadn't found it yet.

"I'll call her," Lily said, heading for the phone.

Chas jumped in her path. "No. She's busy at the diner. Besides," he said, and grinned when inspiration struck. "She thought it might be nice for you to come over tonight and visit."

"Oh," Lily said, stepping back, away from him. "That's kind of sweet."

"It's very sweet. I think you're going to have a really good time tonight."

That evening they drove into the driveway of the bed and breakfast, and Lily noticed that after Chas pulled his keys from the ignition of his car he played with the chain, searching for another key. She didn't say anything, but her brow puckered in confusion when he slid the key into the lock of the front door and opened it for her, granting her entry.

"Thanks," she said, still perplexed, but not so rattled that the scent of roses didn't immediately overwhelm her. "Oh, my! Abby must have some admirer," she said, looking from the foyer into the formal living room which was filled with every color and variety of rose imaginable.

"The roses aren't for Abby," Chas said simply, coming up behind her and sliding her coat from her shoulders.

She swallowed. "They're not?"

"No, they're for you."

"Me?" she whispered, not entirely sure what was going on. A strange tingle overwhelmed her, partly from the surprise of discovering she was the recipient of hundreds of roses, and partly from the way he'd so casually taken her jacket. "But I'm not staying here anymore," she said slowly, "who would send roses to me here?"

"I did," he said simply. "I filled the room with roses because I knew I was bringing you here tonight. I wanted you to feel special."

He said it confidently, with the deep baritone of a man well accustomed to getting his own way, and Lily didn't know whether to be honored or panic-stricken. In the end she decided to stall for time if only to figure out what to do...how to handle herself. "But what about my thing?" she asked stupidly.

"What thing?"

"The thing I was supposed to have left behind," she said, refusing to turn around because if she turned around she'd have to look at him, and she wasn't quite sure she was ready.

"You didn't really leave anything behind. I made that up. I rented the bed and breakfast for the evening so we could have some privacy. I just wanted us to have some time for ourselves, no kids, no phone, no Grant," he said, emphasizing his brother's name. "I didn't even tell Abby the whole story."

"Oh," Lily said, her panic growing, but at least now she knew that what she was feeling was panic. She was alone in a strange house, with a man she'd known about six weeks, and he had not only filled the living room with flowers, he'd arranged it so they'd have hours of uninterrupted, unsupervised time together. After the way he'd kissed her the day before and the way she'd responded and the way their feelings for each other kept growing, she had a sneaking suspicion of why. He expected her to make love with him.

Her limbs froze.

Her brain froze.

The strange tingling turned into frissons of unwanted excitement. If her body had any say in the debate, they'd make love. If her mind had any say, they wouldn't. If her emotions ruled, she didn't have a clue how the night would end.

Still frozen, she stared at the multicolored roses. Twenty vases. Twenty colors. Some variations so slight, it took a keen eye to realize there were differences. But she noticed. And she knew he'd been careful, precise, deliberate.

Her eyes misted. Even as she realized no one had ever done anything so sweet for her before, she also saw that it was a sneaky, low-down male trick. He was counting on the fact that she'd be so overcome with emotion from the gesture that she'd be putty in his hands.

The damnable part of it was, she was just about positive he was right.

"Come on," he said, grabbing her hand. "Our dinner should be done now."

He tugged her down the dimly lit hall of the dark, stately house. She knew from Abby that the motif was part of the attraction that brought back patrons year after year, particularly during the fall when the leaves were turning color and everyone wanted to see the spectacle of the Appalachian Mountains in varying shades of gold, auburn and orange. Abby had explained that there was something about the way a fire heated the dark, drafty house that turned it into a warm, romantic place.

In the chill of the early evening, without the fire, Lily found it hard to believe that these ornate rooms could ever be comfortable, let alone warm. The sharp colors of the stained-glass windows emphasized the cold of the wind howling around the house. Deep-hued, turn-of-the-century rugs were another part of the charm for visitors, but the reserved, austere look didn't do a thing to make Lily believe that this house could ever be considered warm, welcoming, or even slightly friendly.

But she'd just as soon take her chances and believe Abby's story than uncover the truth for herself. If Chas fed her, plied her with wine, then wooed her in front of a crackling fire, she didn't stand a chance. What remained of her innocence would be a distant memory.

In the kitchen he pulled a pot roast from the oven. Potatoes and carrots surrounded the browned meat.

She smiled. "A meal all in one pan," she said, watching as he slid the glass baking dish onto the counter. "And a pan that the food can be served in. You must have to do the dishes."

Occupied with getting their dinner secured, he didn't look at her. "I do."

Why, he's nervous, she realized. As nervous as she was. This time the emotion that tugged at her heart wasn't fear, confusion or even excitement. It was something warm and soft. Not only had he filled a room with flowers and cooked her a meal, but he was anxious about her reaction. Or maybe nervous to be alone with her.

She felt the tug on her heartstrings again and the overwhelming urge to hug him.

Carrying the glass baking dish with hands covered by oven mitts, he led her into the dining room. An intimate seating arrangement for two was set with delicate china and crystal, undoubtedly Abby's, and two tall white candles were strategically placed on either side of one long-stemmed white rose.

Chas didn't turn on the light, Lily assumed, because his hands were full. But when he set the roast on the table, he immediately fished into his pocket, took out matches and lit the candles. They sparked to life, providing an intimate yellow glow to the room, bright enough that they could see only a few feet in either direction.

"Have a seat," he said, pulling out an upholstered, straight-backed chair for her.

Lily held back a shiver. Soft lights, food she didn't have to cook or fuss over, no children, no worries. It all seemed too good to be true.

"Chas, this is really nice." She sat, then swallowed as his hands brushed the back of her shoulders. She felt like a princess or a bride being pampered by her new husband. She felt as if they were the only two people on the planet—the only two people who needed to be on the planet.

A burst of rain pounded against the window, reminding her of the real world that waited outside, and of the very valid possibility that he'd brought her here to seduce her. Because she was wearing jeans, a fuzzy turtleneck sweater and tennis shoes, it was obvious romance had been the last thing on her mind when they'd left Brewster Mansion. But he'd dressed in Dockers, a comfortable pale pink oxford cloth shirt and burgundy sweater. Refined, yet comfortable, he looked like a man who not only suited this ornate, elaborate room, but who was also well accustomed to spoiling and seduction.

He dropped the serving spoon. It made a loud clatter, and before he could catch himself he cursed roundly.

Relieved, Lily smiled. He's nervous, she reminded herself. As nervous as she was. For some strange reason or other that comforted her.

"Chas," she said, knowing that although his intentions were sweet and his nervousness was endearing, seduction had to be out of the question. "I really appreciate all this. I needed some time away from the kids, too, and the roses are magnificent," she said, and without warning her eyes misted again. Adding a pregnant pause to her statement, she reached for her water and took a small swallow, then she smiled at him. He was staring at her with such a combination of hopefulness and longing that her eyes filled with tears again. "Darn it, stop this. You're charming me, and I don't want to be charmed."

He looked at her. "Why not?"

"Because I don't need to be charmed," she said in a rush. "I've never been charmed. Everett never felt the need to charm me."

As soon as she said Everett's name she regretted it. The already quiet room became stone silent. His face expressionless, Chas sat back in his chair. "His mistake."

Lily took a long breath. "I'm sorry. This is a hell of a time to be talking about Everett."

He toyed with his wineglass. "Actually this is the perfect time. You know, you've never really given me the specifics of what happened."

"That's because I don't want to talk about it."

He waited until he caught her gaze. "Maybe you should."

For a man who was trying to seduce her, Lily thought, he was going about it all wrong. The last thing she wanted to do was discuss the most embarrassing moment of her life. "And what would I say?" Lily asked with a half laugh. "That I loved the man and he left me?"

"There's more to it than that. Much more." He caught her gaze again. "I'd like to hear the story."

Dragging in a long draught of air, Lily considered two things. First, if she told him, it would get both their minds off matters of seduction. Second, if she told him, he might not want to seduce her anymore. Either way, she would accomplish the good, right, appropriate purpose. The purpose to which she should be committed whether she wanted to be or not.

She sighed. "Everett was a year older than I was."

"So what was he still doing away at college?"

From his astute question, Lily recognized she'd already told bits and pieces of this story and realized she might as well cut right to the chase. "Postgraduate work in the form of another woman."

Chas peered at her. "Excuse me?"

"Everett said he going to graduate school, but he wasn't. He simply hadn't wanted to return home because our little town was stifling him. He found a job in another city, but rather than tell me he was working, he told me he was attending graduate school because he wasn't ready for me to join him. He wasn't ready to marry me, but he didn't want to give me up, either."

"That should have been a dead giveaway that something was wrong."

"It would have been, if I'd known he wasn't in graduate school," Lily said. "But he told me he was in graduate school, and I never questioned him. I trusted him."

"And now because of your misplaced trust, you don't want to get involved in another relationship."

Surprising even herself, Lily shook her head. "No. That's not how it is at all. But I do know I don't want to be seduced," she said, remembering what Abby and Claire had told her about Chas being spoiled, and theorizing that he might only be interested because she appeared to be something, someone, he couldn't have. "I don't want to be tricked. I don't want to feel that I'm being lied to. If you can't be honest, open and up-front, I don't want to have anything to do with you."

He caught her hand and pulled it to his lips. "Thank God," he said, then pressed a kiss against her palm.

When a starburst of sensations pulsed up her arm, she almost jerked her hand away. The man was going to kill her with desire. There was absolutely, positively no way he could make himself look sweeter, more considerate or sexier than he was right now. If his voice deepened another octave, she'd probably hyperventilate.

"You want to know something?" he whispered, holding her gaze.

She swallowed. "What?"

"I think Everett was a fool."

"Not a fool, just a very confused man who found himself tied to two women. One he'd known forever and couldn't stand to lose…that was me. And another he fell in love with while he was changing, growing up, growing away from me." She smiled in spite of herself. "Remember how I told you he'd sent me a six-page letter, and that we would never see each other again because we didn't need closure?"

Chas nodded.

"He married the other women and took her on my honeymoon. That's why I know I'll never see him again."

"You know, Lily, the more you talk about this guy, the more I think you're lucky to be away from him."

Lily fondled the stem of her glass. "I came to that conclusion myself," she agreed.

"Good, then let's eat before our food gets cold."

The sudden shift in attitude didn't surprise Lily as much as it confounded her. How was she supposed to enjoy dinner, now that she'd talked about Everett? How was she supposed to be happy or even comfortable and relaxed with the most humiliating incident of her life out on the table?

"Peas?"

"Huh?" Lily looked up from the food she'd been shuffling around on her plate and saw Chas offering a serving dish of peas to her. She blinked. "I don't think so."

"I wasn't sure if you'd like the carrots so I made peas just to be sure I'd covered enough vegetables and vitamins."

"In the meal?" she asked, confused.

"Yeah. You know, caring for the triplets has really changed my vantage point on a lot of things, or maybe broadened my horizons. I used to live on fast food. Thought I couldn't survive without it. But we don't have fast food here, and I like to cook." He paused, smiled. "Which is lucky, since there aren't many places for takeout."

She stared at him. "No, there aren't."

"When I was in Philly, I made one meal provide an entire day's calories. First, because I didn't have the money to go overboard on food. And second, because I didn't have enough time to eat, let alone cook."

"Is law school hard?"

"No harder than anything else, I imagine. The results of your life, anybody's life, depend on how much time and effort you want to put in. I wanted to be a really good lawyer. I put in the time, made the sacrifices."

"I want to be something, too."

"Really?" he asked, surprised. "What?"

She shrugged. "I don't know yet. It seems like my whole life revolved around becoming Everett's wife. Now that I can be anything, I want to be careful when I make my choice."

"There are scientifically proven ways to go about picking a career, you know."

"Really?"

"Sure. In the one instance, you divide a piece of paper into three columns. You write your likes down in the first column. In the next column you write down what you don't like. In the last column, you write down what you're good at. Then you start to mix and match and cross things off and pretty soon you end up with a specific set of likes and skills, and you find a job that uses those likes and skills."

"I like people," Lily said thoughtfully. "But I'm best at dealing with women and kids. Men don't treat me fairly. I don't like to work with them." She paused, squeezed her eyes closed. "Sorry. No offense."

"None taken," he said congenially, then speared a potato. "What else do you like?"

"Houses, decorating, entertaining, organizing," she stopped and sighed heavily. "Great. I'm painting myself into the corner of being a housewife again."

"Or a real estate agent."

She glanced at him. "Or a real estate agent," she said, her voice awed with surprise. "A real estate agent."

"I'll bet you'd make a terrific real estate agent."

"You think so?" she asked excitedly.

"Heck, yeah! The liking houses and decorating part is self-explanatory, but I think what you're missing is that there's a lot of organizing that goes into the sale of a house. And it's personal, intimate work. As far as entertaining goes, I'd be willing to bet you'd throw a wicked open house."

She grinned. "I bet I would," she said, but her grin quickly faded. "For all the good it would do me. Brewster County isn't exactly a booming metropolis."

"Not now," Chas said casually. "But you know those two big bids Grant's been working on?"

She nodded.

"They're both for shopping centers. If all goes well, and they get the bids, Grant plans on bringing his company home to do the jobs, but if all doesn't go well, he plans to coerce his partner into coming home anyway to start a housing development. Building a hundred houses is something Grant and Hunter would really sink their teeth into, but selling those houses would be another story. They'd need a sales person."

She frowned. "But does Brewster County need a hundred houses?"

"It will for the people who work at the malls, and all the ancillary stores and businesses the malls will generate. Not to mention the people who are graduating from high school and not leaving, and the people who will return home if there is work for them." Chas paused, took a bite of meat and chewed thoughtfully. "Before it's all over, you could have your own company."

She gaped at him. "I could?"

"You could," he said. This time he stared at her. "You've got to do something about that flagging confidence."

Floating above the clouds on the dream he was creating for her, not feeling in the slightest insecure, Lily giggled. "My confidence isn't flagging, I'm just astounded."

"About what?"

"About being ready to commit myself to a life that was all wrong. I mean, I wanted to be a housewife. I still may be someday. But for now I like the sound of this much better."

"And you're not going to commit yourself to things that are wrong for you anymore?" he asked, and took her hand again.

"No," she said, getting the sudden sensation that he was no longer talking about starting a company.

He brought her fingers to his lips. "Do you like your dinner?"

She swallowed. "Yes. Very much."

"Like the peace and quiet?"

She nodded.

"I'm glad we had this time."

"Me, too," she said, realizing something incredible just occurred. They'd had a wonderful, romantic, sexually charged dinner and nothing had "happened" except that they'd gotten closer. She relaxed. "Me, too," she repeated, smiling at him.

"I actually have the bed and breakfast for the entire weekend," he said, his eyes devilish and teasing. "I don't suppose I could entice you into staying away a little longer?"

She shook her head. "Somehow I don't think that would be wise."

"Finding yourself a little attracted to me?"

"I've always been attracted to you."

His smile grew. "I wasn't sure. You're not easy to read."

Since the situation was harmless and since Chas had more or less declared his intention to follow her wishes, Lily didn't see any harm in being honest. "I find you incredibly attractive. Sweet, sexy and charming. Not just here and now, and not because of the dinner. But every day. *Any* day.''

Pleased, he grinned. "Really?"

"Yeah, but that's as far as we're taking this particular discussion. We're going to do Abby's dishes and head for home. It's not fair to leave Grant alone with the kids."

"Claire and Evan are staying overnight," Chas said hopefully, hinting shamelessly. "Not only do they want to be sure Cody has quality time with the girls, but they want to make sure *they* have enough time with the girls."

"They're sweet," Lily said, pulling her hand away from Chas's two seconds before he would have kissed it again. It was the strangest thing. Now that they were back to normal, the little things, the subtle things, were sexier than the hundreds of clever things he'd done to please her. "Still, I'm not staying."

She pushed her chair back as if to rise, and he was behind her, helping her with her chair before she had fully risen.

She smiled. "Thanks."

"You're welcome," he said, then kissed her. Though it wasn't a long, lingering kiss, it wasn't a quick kiss, either. His mouth pressed on hers for enough time that her thoughts became fuzzy and she nearly put her arms around him.

He pulled away.

She blinked in confusion, but quickly composed herself, because she believed that being this confounded by a man had to be a weakness of some sort. Not that she didn't like it. She did. She liked it too much. So much that she forgot everything but the softness of his lips and the taste of his mouth whenever he kissed her. And that wasn't good. She had to keep her wits about her.

Drawing a life-sustaining breath, she glanced at the table. "You wash. I'll dry."

"Okay," he agreed, and pulled her into his arms. His open mouth fell upon hers with the lightness of a feather and the greediness of a miser, stealing her thoughts, seducing her into responding. His hands roamed down her back and then up again, as restless as his mouth, possessive and ravenous.

Her head tilted back. Her spine arched against his roving palms. She felt small against his size and strength. Feminine against his masculinity. His lips toyed with hers. His hands set out to please her. And she could have happily melted at his feet.

"Stay with me tonight," he whispered against her mouth, his words low and deep, resonating from him and seeping into her.

She knew his longing because she felt it, too. An urgent need swept through her. Her limbs were heavy and weak. Her brain was clouded. And inside she felt a yearning so simple and so pure it humbled her. Everything in her life, everything in her world paled against the thought of giving herself to him. Not just because he needed her, but also because she needed him. Life had boiled down to one basic truth. She'd found the person with whom she wanted to spend the rest of her life. She'd found her mate.

"I'll make a fire. I'll make you happy," he said, sliding his lips down the column of her throat, and Lily swallowed. "I've never wanted to please anyone as much as I do you."

The cotton in her brain seemed to be growing thicker. Rudimentary thought began to elude her. Her limbs refused to move. Warm, wonderful tingles enveloped her, even as his tongue traced the line of the crew neck of her sweater.

"Say you'll stay."

Gulping in air, Lily forced her eyes open. Nothing so complicated had ever seemed so clear, and she knew she couldn't refuse him. But she wanted her eyes open when she gave her agreement and she wanted to be sure she had his full agreement, too. She wanted to know there were no misinterpretations on either part. She wanted to be sure this was an even deal. No seduction. No trickery. After Everett, she promised herself she'd never been fooled by a man again.

"Chas," she said, again gasping for air when his hands slid under the back of her sweater. A sweet burst of arousal coursed through her, but she took a slow calming breath and tried again. "Chas, I'll..."

Before she could get the word *stay* out of her mouth, the hall lights flickered then died away completely. If there hadn't been candles on the table, they would have been in total darkness.

"Did you turn out the lights?" she asked, even as a torrent of rain pummeled the dining room window.

"What lights?" he asked, then nibbled her neck. "I didn't do anything to the lights."

She heard the rain again. A barrage of hard, heavy drops blasted the dense glass behind her. "Do you realize we're getting a storm?"

"It's raining."

"It's more than raining," she insisted, pulling away from him. "There's a storm out there," she said, and went to the glass. It was cold to the touch and the water clinging to the pane looked more like droplets of ice than droplets of liquid.

She pivoted and stared at him. "We're in the middle of an ice storm."

Chapter Eleven

Angry, Lily grabbed a candle, strode to the vanity that served as a check-in desk for visitors and yanked the phone receiver from its cradle.

"I swear. I didn't know we were getting an ice storm," Chas said, following her.

"And you didn't have a clue that we'd be trapped?" Lily accused, putting the receiver to her ear and sighing with disgust when she didn't get a dial tone.

"If the electricity is out," Chas explained, "then the phone is also out. And no, I didn't have a clue we'd be stranded. If I didn't know we were getting a storm, how could I have known we were about to be stranded?" He paused, raked his fingers through his hair. "Look, Lily, I'm sorry."

"I'll bet," she said, bounding away from him and back into the dining room where she began gathering dirty dishes.

He followed her again. "You can't be mad at me for this."

"Really?" she asked sarcastically. "Why not?"

"Because it proves you still don't trust anyone. Me in particular."

Obviously thinking about that, she stopped before pushing through the swinging door into the kitchen. He nearly bumped into her back. But he didn't. And, since he was in so much hot water with her, he also didn't think it prudent to remind her there was no light in the kitchen. Instead, he carried a candle with him.

Hoping he was about to get a reprieve, she disappointed him when she shook her head and said, "Nope. Not buying it."

"Not buying what?" he asked, exasperated.

"That stupid lamebrained excuse you keep tossing at me—that I don't trust anyone."

"If you trusted me, you wouldn't be mad right now."

"I'm not mad because I don't trust you. I'm mad because you *tricked* me. You didn't have to trick me by renting the bed and breakfast on the night of an ice storm. All you had to do was ask me to go with you."

"Yeah, right. Like you would have just come away with me for a night."

"Who says I wouldn't have?"

He stared at her. "You mean you would have?"

She tossed her hands in frustration. "I don't know. I might have. But now we'll never know because you didn't let me have the opportunity to make the choice."

When she marched away again, he scrambled after her. He wanted everything out in the open forever and for good, but she wouldn't stand still long enough to talk about it. And he blamed Everett for that. Because if it hadn't been for Everett they wouldn't be arguing right now. He couldn't help but believe that Everett would stand between them forever. Not only was that stupid man keeping them apart, but now he was even ruining the arguments that might help them resolve an issue or two and allow them to let their relationship go to the place both of them wanted it to be.

Well, this time he wasn't letting her use Everett as a shield any more than he was letting Everett get off scott-free. He might have to fight Everett's fight for him, but he sure as hell wasn't taking his punishment. He was making damn sure the blame got cast exactly where it belonged.

"Are you mad at me, or are you mad at Everett?"

She whirled to face him. "I'm mad at you!"

"I don't think so," he disagreed, pushing past her and setting his dishes and the candle on the counter beside the sink. He grabbed a dishpan, squirted in some soap and started the hot water. "Oh, technically you're angry with me, but the truth is you wouldn't have doubted my intentions for one minute if Everett hadn't given you a reason to mistrust everyone. Face it, kid, you're still not over him."

"Oh, you'd like to believe that's true, wouldn't you?"

He tossed delicate china into the sudsy water. "And you'd like to believe it's not true."

Laughing slightly, she shook her head. "For your information, I washed my hands of him as quickly and easily as I washed this dish," she said, dunking the plate into the water, swiping it clean and rising it. "And do you know why? Because being left at the altar was something like the final straw. He'd left me alone for an entire year. A year. I spent a year hardly seeing him. I got a phone call every week, and a visit every month if I was lucky, but that was it. Though I put my anger and nerves down to prewedding jitters, I now realize that being deserted had worn me down."

Chas stopped washing silverware. This was new, and significant. "You didn't see him for a year?"

Not noticing the relevance of what she'd said, she shook her head. "I got a visit each month, and he came home for every holiday."

Astounded, Chas watched her dry a dish. It was no wonder he had the sense that she hadn't been pampered or spoiled in a long time. It was no wonder he felt her loneliness. It was no wonder he didn't get a sense of pain.

He took a long breath. "This changes everything."

"I can't see how."

"You're in worse shape than I thought."

Her eyes narrowed. "If you accuse me of not being over Everett one more time, I'm going to punch you."

"Save your strength, slugger, because the last thing I'd accuse you of right now is not being over Everett." He delicately slid a serving dish into the water. "The person you're really hooked on is me. And you have been for weeks. Maybe even a month. You just wouldn't let yourself admit it because you thought it wasn't possible to climb out of one relationship and into another. But guess what? You didn't have a relationship with Everett. You broke up a year ago, you just hadn't bothered to tell each other. And you met me and, bingo, that was it. You fell head over heels."

"You're nuts," she sputtered, grabbing a dish to dry.

"I'm right," he said, and kissed her for good measure. "But don't worry, I'll be gentle."

"You're not going to be anything. In the first place, you're wrong, I didn't fall head over heels in love with you," she insisted, but even as the words came out of her mouth, she knew they were lies. Just as he'd said, she'd fought and fought to keep from admitting it be-

cause she didn't believe it was possible. But looking at
the situation from the perspective he just gave, she had
to admit it was true. Not seeing Everett for the past year,
she wasn't merely mad at him, she'd also fallen out of
love with him. Maybe months ago. *Probably* months
ago. And when she'd met Chas Brewster she was ripe
for the picking.

She combed her fingers through her hair. She needed
some time to think about this. Lots of time. More time
than the few hours they'd have to kill before going to
bed.

Bed.

Oh, boy. Now that she knew she'd been out of love
with Everett for months and had every right in the world
to fall in love with Chas, and probably actually had,
sleeping with him was back to being an option.

"Still sorry we're stuck here for the night?"

His voice was smooth and sweet like good whisky.
Confident like the voice of Satan tempting a die-hard
sinner. He felt he had her, and she felt trapped.

She looked him right in the eye. "Yes."

"Ah, come on," he said, splashing water everywhere
when he dropped his hands in dismay. "We are never
going to get another chance like this."

"I don't care," she said, and picked up the serving
dish to wipe it dry. The real truth, the real issue, wasn't
whether or not she'd fallen in love, but whether or not
she'd done so wisely. She'd told herself she would be
wise the next time, but because she hadn't been aware
of being out of love with Everett she didn't fight the
right way to keep herself from falling for Chas. Because
she hadn't fought, she was once again in love and not
quite sure she was supposed to be. Chas Brewster was
spoiled. Abby had come right out and said it, and Claire

had hinted. But instead of being careful, cautious or even slightly prudent, she'd tumbled right in.

At the same time she wasn't entirely sure this had been a mistake. She wasn't convinced Abby was right. Unfortunately she couldn't say Abby was wrong, either. And unless or until she understood exactly what was going on, she wasn't doing anything.

"I get the first bedroom on the right."

He looked over at her. "What?"

"I want the first bedroom on the right. It's where I stayed before and I know where everything is."

"Lily, you're not going to be able to stay in any of the bedrooms," he said, agitated again. "The furnace may still run, but without electricity for the pump, the warm water's not going to be getting into the radiators. We're going to have to sleep in the living room." He paused, smiled. "In front of the roaring fire."

"Oh, yeah, right!" she scoffed, staring at him. "Do I look as if I just fell off a turnip truck?"

"No, you look like a woman who just had a lovely dinner and who is ready to go into the living room and enjoy her flowers while she sits in front of the fire."

The reminder of the flowers stopped her. It was hard to believe that a man who was truly self-centered and spoiled would fill a room with flowers for a woman, but, then again, if the man were truly self-centered and spoiled, he might fill the room just to get the woman where he wanted her.

Oh, she didn't know. And her head was spinning from all the guessing. But more than that, though it hadn't happened fast, the suddenness of her own realizations left her reeling. She felt as if she'd jumped out of the frying pan and into the fire.

"I don't want to be pushed, I don't want to be co-erced, I don't want to be seduced. I want choices."

"I'm paying for Everett's mistakes again, aren't I?"

She sniffed daintily. "Not really. We're just playing by my rules now."

He grabbed her arm and brought her hard up against him, looking directly into her eyes. "Your rules for now, because I want to prove this really was an accident. But we won't always be here. And you won't always get your own way. And this relationship won't stay stagnant for long. A thing either grows or it dies. If you let it die, I think you'll be sorry. If you give it a chance to grow, we both know exactly where we're headed. Your choice. But think about it long and hard because if you let it die I'm not taking the blame, and if you want it to grow you'd better be ready because I'm not like anybody you know."

He let her sleep in the bedroom because she insisted. As he built a fire in the rapidly chilling living room, he muttered to himself. Mostly he called himself every kind of stupid, then he kicked off his shoes and bundled beneath a comforting quilt. Within minutes the blaze brought the room to a fairly decent temperature, and though he knew he should stay awake and alert to keep the fire well stocked with logs, he didn't even try to defend himself against sleep. When his eyelids began to droop, he let them.

Why? Because he was mad. Damn it. He'd gone to a great deal of trouble to make Lily feel special, and all he'd ended up doing was make her feel cheap.

He yawned and burrowed more deeply under his cover. He'd screwed this up royally.

Upstairs Lily piled blanket after blanket on the bed of

her cold, cold room. Out of necessity, she kept on her fuzzy sweater, jeans and even her socks and crawled into her refuge. The sheets were like ice. Even through her clothes she could feel them. She curled into a ball, shivering. But she clenched her mouth closed and slammed her eyes shut. She'd be damned if she'd play right into his hands.

Forcing herself to think of a blue sky filled with billowing white clouds above a grassy meadow in the middle of summer, Lily eventually calmed down enough to relax. She soon warmed up and uncurled from her fetal position.

Before she had a chance to rev herself up again with anger, she fell into an exhausted sleep. But after what seemed like only minutes, she awakened, shivering. In spite of all her precaution, the chill of the room had managed to find her. She decided to ignore it, but in the end had to admit that Mother Nature was a lot stronger than she was. Her teeth were chattering. Her nose was frozen. If she could see them, she'd bet her lips were blue. She tried to muster some pride to save herself, but every time she birthed a good reason to stay in her room the cold air killed it.

On a curse, she rolled out of bed, taking her covers with her, and stomped downstairs. She found Chas lying on the sofa in the living room. The fire was nearly dead. The room was almost as chilly as the one she'd just left.

Angry, she kicked his foot. "Wake up and sit up so I can have some space on the couch."

"What?" he asked, not opening his eyes.

"It's freezing in my room. I need to be down here, and I don't want to sit on the floor."

"Lily?" he asked groggily, his eyes opening a crack.

"You were supposed to be able to keep me warm,"

she accused, kicking at his foot again. "But you let the fire go out, and it's even freezing down here. I might as well go upstairs again."

That brought him to his feet. "I'll rebuild the fire," he said, and immediately went for the small stash of wood off to the right.

Slowly lowering herself to the sofa, she eyed him warily.

He smiled at her. "In ten minutes it'll be warm as toast. Slide over," he said, then plopped beside her when she did.

She eased away.

"You would be warmer if you would leave your blankets and join me under mine."

"I'll bet."

"Come on, Lily," he coaxed. "You know you like me, and we're both freezing. We shouldn't just be taking advantage of each other's warmth, we should be taking advantage of hours and hours of privacy. Privacy we'll never see again," he added honestly.

Shivering, recognizing he was right, and never one to hold a grudge, she rearranged her covers so that he could slide beneath them with her. He wrapped her against his rock-solid chest, and though the warmth that seeped into her had nothing to do at all with body temperature and everything to do with sexual energy, she didn't move. She rested her head against his shoulder, closed her eyes and savored the strength, the heat, the masculinity of him.

Sighing, he put his chin on the crown of her head. "I really am sorry."

His sincerity sent a torrent of confusion through her. She didn't want him to be right about her being in love with him, but she knew she was in love with him. She

knew she had the depth of passion for this man that
could take her through a lifetime. It could take her
through the good times and bad, sickness and health. She
had the sort of love for this man that she'd fancied herself having for Everett, except she could see a much
clearer, much more realistic future with Chas. As real as
the solid muscle and flesh against which she leaned, as
real as the integrity and innate goodness she'd seen
every day in how he lived his life, she saw their future.

"I know that you're sorry," she whispered, but she
was afraid. She knew a future was a very fragile, intan-
gible thing. And Chas was a very unpredictable man.
There was no way she could really judge what he was
thinking, what he was feeling, and she didn't want to
spend her life confused and guessing.

"Do you know that I love you?"

His whispered question floated down to her, and
awed, honored, she pressed her lips together to hold back
a tidal wave of emotion. He loved her. She let the words
and the meaning behind them soak into her soul, let them
cure her of her insecurities and misgivings, let them fill
her with courage. In her heart she knew it was time to
give up the past and all its mistakes.

For both of them.

"I love you, too."

His hands shifted. Ever so lightly he slid them from
her shoulder blades to her waist, and then back up again.
She felt him swallow.

"You do?" he asked quietly, his voice rich and husky
with sentiment.

"You said you knew," she accused softly, too afraid
to move, to breathe, to look at him.

"I had a pretty good guess," he admitted, but this
time there was laughter in his voice.

Her stiff shoulders relaxed a bit. "I didn't really have a clue about you."

He pushed her away slightly until he could look at her. "You're kidding, right?"

Embarrassed, she shook her head. "In the first place you were moody—"

"Trying to protect myself from getting hurt," he corrected.

"In the second, I'd already misinterpreted the feelings of one man, I was trying very hard not to misinterpret a second. And in the third, I've heard you're spoiled. A man who doesn't like to take no for an answer and who frequently goes after things he can't have."

"I'm going to have to have a long talk with Abby and Claire."

Though he was gazing at her as if he didn't really give a damn about what anybody said about him, Lily wasn't about to let this drop without a little more explanation, and she whispered, "Do you go after things you can't have?"

"Always," he admitted, then tipped up her chin and sipped at her lips.

Breathless, she shifted away from his warm, inviting mouth. "I'm serious."

"So am I," he agreed. "Everybody seems to think I can't have you...or *shouldn't* have you...."

"And now you're going after me," she said disappointedly.

He covered her mouth with his and took a long, hungry kiss. When he pulled away, Lily was tingling with arousal and so dazed she could only stare at him.

"The biggest skeptic was me. I'd already made three mistakes," he said, holding her gaze. "*I* told myself I couldn't have you, that I should stay away from you and you convinced me otherwise.'' His eyes turned solemn, questioning. "I trust you, Lily. More than I've ever trusted anyone in my whole life, and I want you...more than I've ever wanted anyone in my whole life.''

Bursts of fire sparked her nerve endings. His honesty and vulnerability told her more than his words and gave her the boldness to lift her hands to his face. Placing her palms against his cheeks, she said, "And I want you more than I've ever wanted anyone in my life. And I trust you.''

Palms pressed to his cheeks, she brought his mouth to hers again. The blanket tumbled from their shoulders and pooled on their laps. Neither noticed nor cared. The fire had delivered comfortable warmth to the room, but neither noticed that, either. Lily was overwhelmed with the truth of how different real, mature love was from the childish infatuation she'd clung to for years.

Chas was immersed in the euphoria of finally, finally finding the woman of his dreams. His future. In a sense it was sad that it had taken someone who'd shared an equal disaster to understand him and love him the way he needed to be loved, but, then again, the logic of it was so perfect it was poetic.

Even as he thought the last, Lily purred against his cheek, promising everlasting love. Entranced in a bubble of pure joy, her comments didn't register at first, but when he realized she was talking as if they were getting married, the bubbles of pure joy became bubbles of pure, unadulterated panic. He pushed her away from him.

"What did you say?'' he asked quietly.

"I asked how you intend to inform your family that we'll be getting married.''

If he hadn't been so overcome with fear, loathing and disbelief, he might have measured his next words more carefully. But because he was swamped in remembered feelings of hopelessness, futility and failure, he said, "I'm not marrying you."

The stricken look on her face astounded him, and he stared at her. "Lily, I can't believe *you* would ever consider getting married, either." Confused, angry, he ran his hand across the back of his neck. "Lily, honey, marriage hasn't been kind to either one of us. I thought you understood that I have no intention of going down that road again. I'll love you forever. I'll take care of you. I would support you, if I thought you couldn't support yourself. I will be yours. Always. Forever. But I will not marry anyone. Not even you."

Chapter Twelve

"I want to stop at the diner for coffee."

Lily stared out the window. "Fine."

"Would you like some coffee?"

No. What she really wanted was to turn back the clock. This morning she had the singular distinction of being rejected twice in her lifetime...in the same year...almost the same month. And why? Because she had a soft heart and a trusting streak that didn't seem to quit, and not enough experience to know how to guide either one of them.

In an ironic way, she understood that fate might have brought her to Brewster County to show her that what she had with Everett wasn't worth grieving over, but in this case it seemed the cure was worse than the problem. What she felt for Chas went so far beyond what she'd felt for Everett that the new pain, the fresh, raw pain currently slicing her into shreds was a hundred times stronger than what she felt over losing Everett.

She didn't understand how someone could love you

and not want to commit to you. From his letter, she could read that Everett loved her. After six years of being together she supposed it would have been hard for him not to love her.

He simply didn't want to marry her.

Now Chas loved her and he didn't want to marry her either.

She was cursed.

Except with this rejection, things were far more complicated than Everett's leaving her at the altar. She loved Chas more than she'd ever believed it possible to love someone; she worked with him; and she needed her job. The equation as it stood didn't work out.

Worse, she loved the triplets. She'd made friends in Abby and Claire. She finally had a real life, not an extension of someone else's life the way she'd had with her sister, not a hoping-for-the-future kind of life as she'd had with Everett, but a life. A real life. If she ran away from the pain of losing Chas the way she'd run away from the pain of losing Everett, she wouldn't have a life again. She would have to start all over.

Which meant she had a choice. Give up everything she'd worked for in the past two months and face the cruel loneliness of beginning again, or try to get over a man who loved her but couldn't marry her—while spending twenty-four hours a day with him.

No matter which road she chose, she was in for pain, suffering and abject misery.

"Actually, I think I need some coffee." Or at least a few more minutes away from Brewster Mansion to try to reason out what to do. She wondered if Chas, too, wasn't stalling for time because he wasn't ready to deal with the consequences of everything that had happened in the past twenty-four hours, but decided it didn't matter. Not only was her choice supposed to be *her* choice, a choice that suited her and her life, but also she had to stop recognizing all the ways they were alike. She had to stop seeing them as a team, as partners. She had to get on with the rest of her life.

At least, she thought, carefully picking her way across the icy sidewalk to the diner door, no one really knew about this. If they gave a convincing enough story to Grant, Evan and Claire, this whole mess really could be put behind them. It could be their little secret. An indiscretion known only to the two of them.

Unfortunately, when they walked into the diner, Chas stopped short, as if he'd seen a ghost. "Abby?" he said, confused. "What are you doing here?"

"I work here," she answered flippantly.

"You were supposed to be—"

"Out of town," Abby agreed cheerfully. "And we were, for about two hours. But when the storm got really bad we came back. Spent the night with Fred and his wife," she added, nodding in the direction of the cook.

All the blood drained from Lily's face. Not only had they forced Abby out, but they'd put her in a position where she had to seek outside accommodations...and involve someone else in this little drama. "Oh, Abby, I'm sorry," she apologized, her voice shaking with anger and misery. Could she make any mistake without the entire world knowing?

"There's no need to be sorry," Abby said. "Everything worked out okay."

"Not hardly," Chas mumbled, striding to the counter. "Could we have two coffees to go?"

Abby looked from Chas to Lily, and Lily felt her face heat with embarrassment. Particularly when Abby leaned over and whispered, "Are you all right?"

"I'm fine," Lily said, just wishing she could crawl in a hole and die.

Abby made short order of getting their coffee, and Lily gratefully ran out into the October sunshine that was warming the streets and quickly melting the ice. Before she reached the car door, however, Chas nudged her with her coffee. "Here."

"Thanks," she muttered indignantly.

"Lily, this isn't going to work if you go home mad."

"What isn't going to work?" she asked smartly, so angry she could chew nails. "Are you too thick-headed to see it's already failed? Because Abby had to spend the night with Fred and his wife, the entire town will soon know we spent the night together."

Stiffening with resentment, Chas said, "We didn't spend the night together in the way you're implying."

"We might as well have," Lily disagreed, opening her arms wide to indicate the entirety of the small, close-knit community. "They *think* we did, and in a town this size that's all that counts."

"You know, for about ten minutes there I thought you might be upset because we can't seem to make this relationship work when we both want it so badly," Chas said, kicked an icy bank and strode around the cab of the sport utility vehicle. "Now, I see you're just concerned about your reputation. Well, I'm sorry. I'm really, really sorry that by this afternoon everybody and their brother is going to know that we were stranded in this storm and that we were alone at the bed and breakfast since Fred's wife will tell everyone Abby and Tyler spent the night with her."

Even as Chas finished the last of his tirade, Lily watched in horror as Arnie Garrett rounded the corner of the diner. From the satisfied smirk that came to his face, Lily knew he'd heard almost everything Chas had said.

"Well, Chas, Lily, if the two of you aren't a sight for sore eyes."

"What do you want, Arnie?" Chas barked angrily.

Arnie smiled. "Absolutely nothing now. In fact, after hearing that you're sleeping with your new nanny, I might even be able to skip getting a Christmas gift this year." He paused long enough to chuckle, then turned to Chas and said, "Have a nice day, Counselor. Looks like I will be seeing you in court after all."

Lily stormed into the foyer of the Brewster home and started back the hall to the kitchen and her quarters. Walking more slowly, Chas was behind her. Before Lily got to the kitchen door, though, Evan and Claire appeared on the spiral stairway.

"Hey, are you two okay?" Evan asked cheerfully.

Lily stopped walking.

Knowing he had to field this, Chas cleared his throat. "Yeah. We got stranded in town, so we stayed at the bed and breakfast."

"We figured something like that happened," Claire said agreeably as she and Evan started down the steps.

"But we have good news," Evan announced. "Grant got a call from a woman in Ohio who saw our ad in the Pittsburgh paper. Seems she's looking to move closer to her daughter, and Brewster County is only an hour's drive away. She's coming here Monday for an interview, but Grant talked with her for over two hours, and he thinks she's the perfect housekeeper."

Chas looked at Lily.

Lily looked at Chas.

"No kidding," Chas said uncertainly.

"No kidding," Evan said, joining Chas in the foyer.

But Chas couldn't release Lily's gaze. He saw her go through an analysis of the situation and knew the conclusion she was drawing. Not quite sure why he was making things easy for her, he said, "We had a little excitement ourselves this morning. We ran into Arnie Garrett at the diner. He thinks that because Lily and I stayed in town together we must have slept together. Lily thinks he's going to be filing for custody."

Lily gave him a narrow-eyed look, but Evan cursed roundly. "You mean that just because he thinks you're sleeping together, he's going to be able to accuse you of being incompetent?"

"Or immoral. Which translates into being a harmful influence on the kids."

"That's why your news of a housekeeper couldn't have come at a more perfect time," Lily said, catching Chas's gaze again, as if sending him the message that because he'd opened the door for her she was walking through. "Since Mr. Garrett sees me as some sort of corrupting influence on the triplets, I think it's for the best that I leave so his ammunition is worthless."

"What?" Claire and Evan gasped simultaneously.

Lily swallowed, and Chas could see she was losing her courage. He almost stepped in to contradict her, to stop her, but couldn't get his mouth to form the words, not because she'd hurt him—though she had—but because they were at cross purposes.

He should have realized a woman like Lily would need to be married. He shouldn't have made the assumptions he'd made. Especially since she was so young. But he loved her, and he was blinded by it. Hell, he wasn't blinded by it, he was floored by it. So needy and so raw he would have done anything, said anything,

to get her to love him, too. He'd never admit to deliberately acting selfishly, but he would agree that his own
needs prodded him to see things from the wrong perspective.

So he wouldn't contradict her, wouldn't argue with
her, wouldn't try to get her to change her mind.

But he also wasn't so strong that he could help her,
either. If she really wanted to leave, she'd do it of her
own volition. Hell, wasn't that what she kept saying she
wanted? Choices. Well, if she was making one, she was
making it alone.

When she spoke, her voice shook, and Chas had to
ball his hands into fists to keep himself from reacting.

"I think I should leave. If you're getting a housekeeper, you really don't need me and, frankly, one scandal per lifetime is enough for me. I know my personal
scandal happened in Wisconsin and this is Pennsylvania,
but the effects are the same. I just can't go through this
again."

With that she turned and raced through the kitchen,
but even as Chas lost the tight hold he had on his emotions and started to go after her, Evan caught his arm.
"You didn't really push her into another scandal, did
you?"

"No, damn it!" Chas said, shoving his fingers through
his hair. Once again, he was the bad Brewster. The one
in the wrong. As always, his brother jumped to the conclusion that he'd done something he should be ashamed
of.

"I didn't do anything."

"Then why is she so sure Arnie Garrett's going to
turn this thing in his favor?" Claire asked quietly.

"Because he can," Chas answered simply. "He said
he can, and we all know he will," he added, closing his

eyes and suppressing the anger, the futility, the hope-lessness that flooded him. "Because it looks bad, and sometimes that's all it takes to sway a jury."

Claire glanced at the door through which Lily had just run, then back to Chas again. "You're not going after her?"

"No," Chas said and walked away.

As Lily packed her small suitcase that night, there was a knock at her door. Fearing that it was Chas and know-ing she simply couldn't face him, she said, "Who is it?"

"It's Grant. I'm unarmed, except for a dark-eyed little girl who has missed you."

Lily pressed her lips together and squeezed her eyes shut. "I'm not letting you in unless you intend to fight fair."

Grant opened the door, anyway. "Damn it, Lily, I can't fight fair. If I fight fair, I'll lose. I had to bring at least one baby to even the scales."

Lily took bright-eyed Taylor from Grant's arms. "You're not changing my mind."

"I'd like to, but I decided to respect your wishes. So the best I could do is ask what happened, see if you need a shoulder to cry on, and exploit every damned thing you tell me," he said sincerely. "I would even consider offering to ask my brother to move to Philadelphia."

"You can't separate Chas from the triplets," Lily said emotionlessly, though inside, sensations and feelings churned through her. Chas would have made a wonder-ful father, but he will never be a father. She wondered if he'd considered that, then realized it might be the rea-son he was so close to the triplets. "He adores them, and they love him."

"I know," Grant agreed, roaming the room, inspecting her things. "Odd how he's the one who ended up spending the most time with them when he's the one all of us thought had no common sense, no desire for stability and not one whit of responsibility."

"He has lots of common sense. He wants stability— on his own terms. And he's the most responsible person I've ever met."

"Then what in the name of God did the two of you fight about?"

Unexpectedly pleased, Lily hid a smile by brushing her lips across Taylor's shiny black hair. "He won't tell you, will he?"

"Not a blasted word. Said something about respecting your privacy."

The thoughtfulness of it almost got to her, but she crushed the impulse to forgive him before it gained any strength. "My last romantic problem got a little too public," Lily said, if only because she needed to keep herself focused. "I appreciate him keeping this problem to himself."

"Did he hurt you?" Grant asked, narrow-eyed. "Because if he hurt you, I can still whip the tar out of him."

"He only hurt my heart...and my pride."

"I could whip the tar out of him for that," Grant insisted, prowling the room, still examining her things.

"And it wouldn't do any good. Besides, I don't want him whipped. I think he's suffered enough, too."

Studying a ceramic ballerina, Grant said, "I suppose." He turned, angled the figurine toward her. "You make this?"

"Most of the things you see in this room I made."

"You're very talented."

"Thanks."

"Are you going to do something like this when you move on?"

She shook her head. "No. Actually, Chas more or less pointed me down the path I want to take."

Confused, but impressed, Grant faced her. "Really?"

"He's not completely self-centered and egotistical. He's actually a very nice guy. A good person with a good heart. When I explained I wanted to make something of my life, we more or less examined my options, and he thought I'd make a good real estate agent. Even suggested I talk with you about selling homes you might be building, if the thing with the mall doesn't work out."

"Even if the bids for the mall work out, Hunter and I might go forward with the housing development," Grant said thoughtfully. "There's always been something of a housing shortage in this area, with the new mall it will simply be more obvious."

"And you would need help selling these houses?"

"Absolutely," Grant said, confused. He peered at her. "You'd stay in Brewster County for that?"

Lily sighed. "I'd like to stay in Brewster County because I've made friends. I've started a life here. I've talked with Abby and we came to an agreement about me working as a waitress with her at the diner and getting a discount rate at the bed and breakfast while I pursue my license. I haven't actually checked into schools or anything yet, but it would probably work."

"Yeah," Grant agreed quietly. "It sounds like it would. But will you be happy?"

"I don't know, Grant. But not for the reasons you think. I don't know if I'll ever be happy because I can't remember happy. I thought I found happiness with your brother." She paused, smiled. "I *definitely* found happiness with your brother. We shared so many stupid, wonderful things. We changed diapers together. We shared the misery of our pasts. We talked about lessons we'd learned. We connected. *That* felt like happy."

"It sounds like happy," Grant agreed quietly.

"And it's also gone. Much as I love your brother and knew we'd be very, very good together, it's gone. So, I don't know if I can be happy here. I don't know if happy exists. I do know that I like having friends. I like the purpose I'm finding for my life. For a while happiness can take a back seat."

Smiling ruefully, Grant took Taylor from Lily's arms. "Got it all figured out, have you?"

Uncertain of his point, Lily nodded.

"Good. Good for you, anyway, because you've convinced me that you know what you're doing, and I'm not the kind who stands in anybody's way." He walked to the door, Taylor on his arm, but before he left he glanced over his shoulder at her. "You're sure you're going to be okay without being happy?"

She nodded. "Since my parents died seven years ago, I've done very well without it." She shrugged. "Who knows? Maybe some of us aren't meant to be happy. As long as I'm content and stable, I'm okay."

When she entered the kitchen the next morning, she was carrying her suitcase. Evan, Claire and Grant briefly glared accusingly at Chas. He adroitly ignored them.

"Going to the bed and breakfast already?" Claire asked lightly.

"Grant said Mrs. Romani can be here tomorrow. I wanted the room cleared for her."

"I'd like to keep the room open for you," Grant began, but Chas interrupted him.

"We'd like to keep the room open for you, but we

won't hold you back. Your plans are sound. You're intelligent and strong. You'll be fine."

Grant glared at him, Evan scowled at him, and Claire gave him a downright hateful look, but Chas ignored that, too. "We do want you to know, though, that if you need anything, *anything,* any one of us would be happy to help you."

"Thank you," she said politely, cheerfully, then picked up her suitcase again. "I guess I'll see you in town at the diner."

"You're going *now?*" Grant asked incredulously.

"Without coffee even?" Evan seconded.

Smiling uncomfortably, Lily nodded.

"I'll walk you to the door," Claire offered, jumping from her chair.

"*I'll* walk her to the door," Grant contradicted, lightly pushing Claire back down again.

"*I'll* walk her to the door," Chas said, slipping around Grant. "And everybody else stay exactly where you are. This is between Lily and me."

Lily knew she shouldn't get her hopes up. She knew that if he wanted her to stay he wouldn't have carried her suitcase to her car for her. She also knew that if he'd changed his mind about marriage, he wouldn't look sad. But irrational hope skittered through her, anyway.

He tossed her suitcase in the back seat of her car, then opened the driver's side door for her.

Shoving his hands into the front pockets of his jeans, Chas watched a spot on the driveway as he said, "I just wanted to apologize one more time. For everything."

Angry, infuriated, she gaped at him. "You can stop your worthless apologizing. I'm not some charity case. I will get by."

His head snapped up. "I know you will. I'm sorry."

She glared at him. "Stop apologizing!"

"Okay. All right," he said, and almost apologized again, but seemed to pull his words back before he did. "I know you will be fine, but I also want you to know that I'll check up on you."

Her glare turned into absolute fury. "Over my dead body. I don't even want to *see* you again."

Her anger seemed to penetrate his neutral state, and his eyes narrowed, as if he, too, had become irritated. "You know, you keep pushing at me as if I've done something horrible, but I didn't. I don't like the fact that we had a misunderstanding any more than you do, but the truth is we are at cross purposes."

"Yes, you're right," Lily said, attempting to slide into her seat, but he stopped her.

"You're getting sanctimonious."

"All I'm trying to do is get out."

He realized then that he was keeping her from going, holding her back when he should be letting her go, and he stepped away from her car.

After she slammed her door and settled herself on the seat, he watched her draw a long breath, then unexpectedly lower her window. Even before the hope that she had changed her mind about marriage had a chance to spring to life, he crushed it. She was too young to commit to someone who refused to marry. If he'd taken her age into consideration weeks ago, things wouldn't have progressed as far as they had.

Neither one of them would be hurting right now.

Shielding her eyes from the sun, she said, "Chas, don't forget to call Arnie Garrett. He doesn't have a leg to stand on again since I'm moving out of the house and out of your life."

Her words ripped through him, but he smiled ruefully. "See, good things come to those who wait."

She gave him her own version of a rueful smile, yanked the gearshift of her car into drive and jammed her foot onto the accelerator.

He'd never expected that this would be easy. He'd never expected that it wouldn't hurt to watch her go.

What rankled was the sudden, distinct feeling he got that he was wrong. That he was doing something wrong or had done something wrong. And he hadn't. He'd stopped them from making the biggest mistake of their lives.

And now he had to be strong enough to *keep* them from making the biggest mistake of their lives, because every cell in his body wanted to call her back.

Chapter Thirteen

Looking for peace, quiet and privacy that night, Chas sneaked away to the den. He retrieved the bottle of twelve-year-old scotch that had been his father's and poured himself three fingers over ice. When he took the first sip, he closed his eyes and let the heat of the alcohol sear through him, but it wasn't enough. When he opened his eyes again, he was still in the den of Brewster Mansion, still custodian of a baby and partial custodian of another two, still a struggling lawyer.

Still alone.

"You busy?"

When he saw Grant in the doorway, Chas almost lied and told him that he was too busy for company right now. Since he not only had an open bottle of scotch on his desk, but also had a glass in his hand, Chas knew fibbing wasn't an option.

"Resting," he admitted.

"Can I come in?"

Chas combed his fingers through his hair. "Yeah, sure. Why not? Want a drink?"

"No. Hell, no," Grant said as if the scotch were poison. "I have baby duty tonight."

"Claire and Evan going back into town?"

"Yeah, I kind of forced them out. They're newlyweds for God's sake, and we have them spending all their free time with us."

From the way Grant made the simple statement it was hard for Chas not to catch the drift of his meaning. But more than that, Chas could also see the strain all this had put on Grant. Though everyone pulled their weight, Grant was the one who was always thinking. And just as Grant had seen more with Evan and Claire than Chas had seen, he was also the one making the hard decisions about nannies, housekeepers and schedules. He had a knack for taking care of everybody and everything—the same way their father had.

In fact, now that he thought about it, Grant didn't merely have their father's personality, he also seemed to have adopted many of his habits, too.

As if needing to pace, Chas rose from his chair. The official Brewster seat of command. Sure enough, Grant casually took it. But when he sat, sighing as he sank into the worn burgundy leather, Chas suddenly saw how tired Grant looked.

"Maybe I should take night duty?" Chas offered casually.

Grant blew his breath out on a long sigh and refused him. "It's my turn."

"So, we'll shake things up a bit and make it my turn tonight."

"Are you trying to tell your older brother that he can't handle this, little buckeroo?"

"Maybe," Chas said with a laugh. It had been twenty years since Grant had used that nickname, and hearing it brought back so many memories he could have happily sat on the worn leather sofa and bawled like a baby.

Grant leaned back on the tall-backed chair and closed his eyes. "Where has the time gone, Chas?"

"I don't know," Chas said, took a slow sip of his scotch and really did begin to pace. "I just don't know."

"It seems like only yesterday I was in this very room fighting with Dad about how I didn't want to work at the mill or live in Brewster County, but wanted to make my own way in life."

Chas chuckled. "Me, too."

"And he gave me the speech about family and loyalty and sticking by your friends."

Chas smiled ruefully. "Me, too."

"And here we are, doing exactly what he wanted us to do fifteen years ago." Grant opened his eyes long enough to pierce his younger brother with a stare. "We should have just listened."

"Yeah," Chas said, then sat on the arm of the sofa. "God, how different my life would be now, if I'd never left home."

"No marriage, no near miss with bankruptcy, no jail," Grant said, then he grinned. "You're damned right your life would have been different." He paused long enough to shake his head, then said, "I'll never figure out what you saw in any of those women."

"I was very attracted to every one of those women."

"But you didn't see the future."

Knowing it was true and there was no sense denying it, Chas shook his head. "Nope."

"And what do you see with Lily?"

Chas shrugged as if he didn't care, but pain ricocheted

through him. This was the last thing he wanted to be talking about right now. "I don't know."

Grant wouldn't let him get away with that. "Of course you know. I can see from the look in your eyes that you know. What did you see with Lily?"

Chas drew a quick breath. "I saw a long time. Probably forever." He shrugged and tried to walk away as if pain wasn't sluicing through him. "I don't know."

Though Chas expected Grant to jump on that, he didn't. In fact, for several seconds he didn't say a word. Just when Chas felt his prayers had been answered, that his family was going to let him alone so he could lick his wounds in peace, Grant asked, "Do you think we didn't notice that you didn't marry Gretchen?"

Confused, Chas faced him. "What the hell does Gretchen have to do with anything?"

"She's the key to this," he said, shifting on Norm Brewster's worn burgundy leather chair. "After Jennifer came Charlene. You married both of them."

Wary, but knowing he wasn't going to be able to live with Grant unless he listened, Chas nodded his acceptance of that fact.

"But after Charlene you never married Gretchen. Which is the key to this whole issue."

Irritated now, Chas sighed. "You think so, huh? All you're doing is proving my point, Grant. Not marrying Gretchen proves I learned my lesson about getting married."

Smiling superiorly, Grant shook his head slowly to the left, then to the right. "No, you learned your lesson about marrying the wrong person."

"I never thought Charlene was the wrong person. I *loved* Charlene," he said, leaning across the desk and getting into Grant's face. "I loved her and love wasn't enough."

"Maybe not that time. But you didn't see forever with Gretchen and you didn't marry her. You learned your lesson. You know the difference between love and lust."

Suddenly seeing the point Grant was making, Chas stilled for a second but shrugged and paced away again. "That doesn't change the fact that love isn't enough."

"Sure it does," Grant said simply, subtly shifting the scotch bottle away and into the bottom drawer of the desk when Chas finished his drink. "You loved Charlene, but did Charlene love you?"

"Of course she did," Chas said, pacing toward the bookcases again.

"You're sure?"

Chas sighed. "Yes. I'm sure."

"She loved you the way Lily loves you?" Grant continued.

"Yes!" Chas said, but in his heart when he really compared Charlene to Lily, not only did Charlene's feelings pale in comparison to what he knew Lily felt for him, but *his* feelings paled in comparison to what he felt for Lily.

Suddenly weak, he almost wished he could sit, but stood frozen.

"What you have isn't average or normal," Grant said quietly. "What you had with Charlene was love...real love," Grant agreed simply. "That probably would have lasted a lifetime if your circumstances had been consistently good. But real life isn't consistently good. We get hard times," he said, catching Chas's gaze. "And challenges," he added, nodding toward the play yard. "And it's a rare woman who can love you, satisfy you and accept you exactly as you are."

"I'm broke," Chas said quietly, then he swallowed. "I've been divorced twice. I have a child and a piece of two more. I don't have a damned thing to offer her."

"You're a Brewster," Grant said, sounding so much like their father that Chas peered over at him. "Not only do you own a stake in this county but you have a responsibility to it. You know the law, you have an education. Someday you're going to be everything you want to be and more. But, stupid as it seems, you're exactly what Lily wants right now. She doesn't care that you're broke. She doesn't care about your past. And she's ready to share your future."

He paused, waited until he caught Chas's gaze again. "You going to throw that away?"

It took Chas until three o'clock in the morning to gather his courage, but once it was gathered he knew there wasn't any turning back. Fingering the key to the front door of the bed and breakfast, he debated knocking, but didn't want to disturb Abby any more than he wanted to get Abby involved in his discussions with Lily. So, he slid the key in the lock, tiptoed upstairs and let himself into the first bedroom on the right.

Sure enough, Lily lay sound asleep in the four-poster bed.

Without any thought for protocol or consequences, he slid his arms beneath her and scooped her out of bed. She snuggled against his chest, and for a minute he actually believed she might sleep through the trip down the steps, out the door and to Brewster Mansion, but as if suddenly realizing that the fabric of his jacket didn't match that of her pillow, she jerked awake.

Unfortunately, when she realized she was being carried, she screamed.

"Shh!" Chas said frantically.

She swatted him. "I'll shh you! What the hell do you think you're doing?"

"Yeah, what the hell do you think you're doing?" Abby asked from behind. When he turned to look at her, he saw she was holding a baseball bat. From the gleam in her eyes, he knew she wasn't afraid to use it.

"I need to talk to Lily."

"So, you just kidnap her?" Abby asked incredulously.

"I wasn't really kidnapping her."

Confused, Abby stared at him. "Then what would you call it?"

"Yeah, what would you call it?" Lily agreed.

"Picking you up for a date?" Chas asked hopefully.

Abby groaned. Lily swatted his shoulder again. "Put me down."

"Will you talk to me?"

At his earnest request, Lily felt herself weakening, but Abby stepped up to the plate with her ball bat. "Do you *want* to talk to him?" she asked forbiddingly.

Before Lily got the chance to answer, Tyler walked into the room, rubbing his sleep-swollen eyes. "Mom?"

"What, honey?" Abby asked, immediately stooping to his height.

"What's happening?"

"Nothing," Abby said, glaring at Chas. "Come on, I'll tuck you into bed again." Because Tyler left the room before her, she turned and said, "I'll be back."

"Don't," Chas said, exasperated.

"Yeah, Abby, you don't have to. I'll settle this."

"You're sure?" Abby asked, brandishing the bat again.

Lily stifled a laugh. "Yeah, I'm sure. But, Abby, if I were you I'd get his key."

Without any further encouragement, Abby marched over to Chas, palm open.

Chas slid Lily to the floor, took his key chain from his pocket, extricated her key and handed it to her. "Sorry."

Abby only glared at him, then left the room.

"You're never going to lose your reputation of being the bad Brewster if you continue to pull stunts like this one."

"That's exactly why I want you to come home with me. I need somebody to keep me on the straight and narrow."

Realizing they weren't going to exchange any pleasantries, but get right to the matter at hand, Lily backed away from him. She couldn't let a cute stunt ruin her resolve. "If you're just looking for someone to keep you in line, you don't need me. I'm sure Grant will be happy to oblige."

At the mention of his brother's name, Chas became thoughtful for a few seconds. "Grant really likes you."

"I know."

Chas shook his head. "No, I mean *really* likes you. He respects you."

Disappointed, Lily only looked at him. "And that's why you're here?"

"Actually, yes," Chas said, as if only figuring that out for himself.

Lily deflated like a cheap balloon. "Well, this one was easy. I expected I'd have to put up a little bit more of a fight to get rid of you. At the very least, I thought you'd make me wish I could go with you. But if you're here because of Grant, save your breath."

Still thoughtful, Chas studied her. "But I am here because of Grant. And I'm not going to pretend I'm not."

Lily peered at him. "Are you okay?"

Unexpectedly, Chas began to laugh. "Yeah. Yeah, I'm really okay." He paused, combed his fingers through his hair. "I'm really, really okay."

If she hadn't been so curious, she might have kicked him out of her room. But because he was acting as if he'd just made an amazing discovery, Lily crossed her arms on her chest and waited. When it seemed as if Chas had pulled himself together, he faced her again, smiled and said, "I love you, you know."

She nodded. "I know."

"And I want to marry you."

"Pay attention to what you're saying, here, Chas, because if I weren't an honorable woman you'd end up with wife number three, and then you'd be miserable again."

"You have plans to make me miserable?"

"No," she said saucily. "I'm not the problem. You are."

"I don't have any problems."

Lily shook her head. "Yes, you do. Mental problems," she said, taking his arm and directing him to her bedroom door. "Go home. Get a good night's sleep. I promise I'll talk to you in the morning."

He turned around and had his hands on her shoulders before Lily even realized he was moving. "But I don't want to talk in the morning. I don't want to talk at all. I want to marry you."

His words cut through her. "Chas, now you're pushing me, and pretty soon you're going to make me mad."

But Chas shook his head frantically. "I see the future with you, Lily. The future. Grant made me see I wanted to marry you. He also showed me that there was a big difference between you and my failed relationships. With you, I see the future.''

Lily froze. "All right," she said. "That's enough. I can put up with a little hysteria from anybody, but now you're not playing fair. You're making me believe some of the things you're saying, and tomorrow when you change your mind, I'm going to hurt again.''

"But I'm not going to change my mind tomorrow," he said urgently. "That's what Grant was trying to show me. I'm not going to change my mind tomorrow." He slid his hands to her cheeks. "I'm not going to change my mind *ever*. I love you. *I love you,*" he said again, this time as if it were the first time he'd ever said the words.

She didn't try to stop him as he slowly lowered his mouth to hers. Not because she believed him, but because she was mesmerized by what he'd said and how he'd said it. The truth was, for every bit as much as it sounded as if he was saying the words for the first time, it felt like she was *hearing* the words for the first time, even though Everett had said them hundreds of times.

When she pulled away from him and gazed into his eyes, she knew he was sensing the same things she was. She licked her suddenly dry lips. "I love you, too," she whispered, overcome by the odd sensation again. She felt as if she heard the quiet click as one door of her life closed, and the soft swish as another door of her life opened. "I love you, too," she said, fascinated, giddy.

"I'm not sure what happened here," Chas said, his palms still pressed to her cheeks. "But I think we just made a lifetime commitment.''

Astounded, she blinked up at him. "I know we did.''

Lily didn't realize Chas had any doubts about her until

he sagged with relief. "Good, thank God," he said, then kissed her. "Let's get your things together and go home."

Though Lily genuinely believed in her heart that she'd made a commitment and he'd made a commitment, she unexpectedly felt shy. Or maybe Victorian. In the updated room of the old, stately house, she suddenly believed that it was important for her to wait. It was important for *them* to wait.

"I'm not coming back with you."

"What?"

She drew in a long, life-sustaining breath. "I said, I'm not coming back with you."

He stared at her. "Why not?"

"Because if we've genuinely made a lifetime commitment, waiting to sleep together for a few weeks won't matter." Oddly inspired, she glanced around the room, looking for the spirit or intelligence that might be guiding her, but realizing the thoughts were coming from her own heart. "It might even be a good thing."

"Waiting?" he echoed, stupefied.

"Yeah," Lily said, confident now that she had her bearings. "Waiting. I love you. I think you're worth waiting for."

It seemed to take a whole minute for Chas to catch on to what she was saying, but once he did, he smiled. "Yeah, I think you're worth waiting for, too."

* * * * *

*Don't miss Grant's story as he, too, finds love in
OH, BABIES!—available in March 2000,
only from Silhouette Romance.*

Soldiers of Fortune...prisoners of love.

Back by popular demand, international bestselling
author **Diana Palmer's** *daring and*
dynamic Soldiers of Fortune *return!*

Don't miss these unforgettable
romantic classics in our
wonderful 3-in-1
keepsake collection.
*Available in April 2000.**

And look for a **brand-new** Soldiers of Fortune tale in May.
Silhouette Romance presents the next book in
this riveting series:

MERCENARY'S
WOMAN

(SR #1444)

She was in danger and he fought to protect her. But
sweet-natured Sally Johnson dreamed of spending forever
in Ebenezer Scott's powerful embrace. Would she walk
down the aisle as this tender mercenary's bride?

Then in January 2001, look for THE WINTER SOLDIER
in Silhouette Desire!

Available at your favorite retail outlet.
**Also available on audio from Brilliance.*

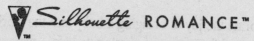

SILHOUETTE'S 20ᵀᴴ ANNIVERSARY CONTEST
OFFICIAL RULES
NO PURCHASE NECESSARY TO ENTER

1. To enter, follow directions published in the offer to which you are responding. Contest begins 1/1/00 and ends on 8/24/00 (the "Promotion Period"). Method of entry may vary. Mailed entries must be postmarked by 8/24/00, and received by 8/31/00.

2. During the Promotion Period, the Contest may be presented via the Internet. Entry via the Internet may be restricted to residents of certain geographic areas that are disclosed on the Web site. To enter via the Internet, if you are a resident of a geographic area in which Internet entry is permissible, follow the directions displayed on-line, including typing your essay of 100 words or fewer telling us "Where In The World Your Love Will Come Alive." On-line entries must be received by 11:59 p.m. Eastern Standard time on 8/24/00. Limit one e-mail entry per person, household and e-mail address per day, per presentation. If you are a resident of a geographic area in which entry via the Internet is permissible, you may, in lieu of submitting an entry on-line, enter by mail, by hand-printing your name, address, telephone number and contest number/name on an 8"x 11" plain piece of paper and telling us in 100 words or fewer "Where In The World Your Love Will Come Alive," and mailing via first-class mail to: Silhouette 20ᵗʰ Anniversary Contest, (in the U.S.) P.O. Box 9069, Buffalo, NY 14269-9069; (In Canada) P.O. Box 637, Fort Erie, Ontario, Canada L2A 5X3. Limit one 8"x 11" mailed entry per person, household and e-mail address per day. On-line and/or 8"x 11" mailed entries received from persons residing in geographic areas in which Internet entry is not permissible will be disqualified. No liability is assumed for lost, late, incomplete, inaccurate, nondelivered or misdirected mail, or misdirected e-mail, for technical, hardware or software failures of any kind, lost or unavailable network connection, or failed, incomplete, garbled or delayed computer transmission or any human error which may occur in the receipt or processing of the entries in the contest.

3. Essays will be judged by a panel of members of the Silhouette editorial and marketing staff based on the following criteria:

   > Sincerity (believability, credibility)—50%
   >
   > Originality (freshness, creativity)—30%
   >
   > Aptness (appropriateness to contest ideas)—20%

   Purchase or acceptance of a product offer does not improve your chances of winning. In the event of a tie, duplicate prizes will be awarded.

4. All entries become the property of Harlequin Enterprises Ltd., and will not be returned. Winner will be determined no later than 10/31/00 and will be notified by mail. Grand Prize winner will be required to sign and return Affidavit of Eligibility within 15 days of receipt of notification. Noncompliance within the time period may result in disqualification and an alternative winner may be selected. All municipal, provincial, federal, state and local laws and regulations apply. Contest open only to residents of the U.S. and Canada who are 18 years of age or older, and is void wherever prohibited by law. Internet entry is restricted solely to residents of those geographical areas in which Internet entry is permissible. Employees of Torstar Corp., their affiliates, agents and members of their immediate families are not eligible. Taxes on the prizes are the sole responsibility of winners. Entry and acceptance of any prize offered constitutes permission to use winner's name, photograph or other likeness for the purposes of advertising, trade and promotion on behalf of Torstar Corp. without further compensation to the winner, unless prohibited by law. Torstar Corp and D.L. Blair, Inc., their parents, affiliates and subsidiaries, are not responsible for errors in printing or electronic presentation of contest or entries. In the event of printing or other errors which may result in unintended prize values or duplication of prizes, all affected contest materials or entries shall be null and void. If for any reason the Internet portion of the contest is not capable of running as planned, including infection by computer virus, bugs, tampering, unauthorized intervention, fraud, technical failures, or any other causes beyond the control of Torstar Corp. which corrupt or affect the administration, secrecy, fairness, integrity or proper conduct of the contest, Torstar Corp. reserves the right, at its sole discretion, to disqualify any individual who tampers with the entry process and to cancel, terminate, modify or suspend the contest or the Internet portion thereof. In the event of a dispute regarding an on-line entry, the entry will be deemed submitted by the authorized holder of the e-mail account submitted at the time of entry. Authorized account holder is defined as the natural person who is assigned to an e-mail address by an Internet access provider, on-line service provider or other organization that is responsible for arranging e-mail address for the domain associated with the submitted e-mail address.

5. Prizes: Grand Prize—a $10,000 vacation to anywhere in the world. Travelers (at least one must be 18 years of age or older) or parent or guardian if one traveler is a minor, must sign and return a Release of Liability prior to departure. Travel must be completed by December 31, 2001, and is subject to space and accommodations availability. Two hundred (200) Second Prizes—a two-book limited edition autographed collector set from one of the Silhouette Anniversary authors: Nora Roberts, Diana Palmer, Linda Howard or Annette Broadrick (value $10.00 each set). All prizes are valued in U.S. dollars.

6. For a list of winners (available after 10/31/00), send a self-addressed, stamped envelope to: Harlequin Silhouette 20ᵗʰ Anniversary Winners, P.O. Box 4200, Blair, NE 68009-4200.

Contest sponsored by Torstar Corp., P.O. Box 9042, Buffalo, NY 14269-9042.

ENTER FOR
A CHANCE TO WIN*

Silhouette's 20th Anniversary Contest

Tell Us Where in the World
You Would Like *Your* Love To Come Alive...
And We'll Send the Lucky Winner There!

Silhouette wants to take you wherever
your happy ending can come true.

Here's how to enter: Tell us, in 100 words or less,
where you want to go to make your love come alive!

In addition to the grand prize, there will be 200
runner-up prizes, collector's-edition book sets
autographed by one of the Silhouette anniversary
authors: **Nora Roberts, Diana Palmer,
Linda Howard** or **Annette Broadrick.**

DON'T MISS YOUR CHANCE TO WIN!
ENTER NOW! No Purchase Necessary

Where love comes alive™

Name:

Address:

City: State/Province:

Zip/Postal Code:

Mail to Harlequin Books: **In the U.S.:** P.O. Box 9069, Buffalo, NY
14269-9069; **In Canada:** P.O. Box 637, Fort Erie, Ontario, L4A 5X3

*No purchase necessary—for contest details send a self-addressed stamped envelope to:
Silhouette's 20th Anniversary Contest, P.O. Box 9069, Buffalo, NY, 14269-9069 (include
contest name on self-addressed envelope). Residents of Washington and Vermont may
omit postage. Open to Cdn. (excluding Quebec) and U.S. residents who are 18 or over.
Void where prohibited. Contest ends August 31, 2000.

PS20CON_R